A Midnight Pastry Shop Called Hwawoldang

LEE ONHWA

Translated by Slin Jung

MICHAEL JOSEPH

PENGUIN MICHAEL JOSEPH

UK | USA | Canada | Ireland | Australia
India | New Zealand | South Africa

Penguin Michael Joseph is part of the Penguin Random House group of companies whose addresses can be found at global.penguinrandomhouse.com

Penguin Random House UK,
One Embassy Gardens, 8 Viaduct Gardens, London SW11 7BW

penguin.co.uk

Penguin
Random House
UK

First published in South Korea as 시간이 멈춰 선 화과자점, 화월당입니다 by
Big Fish Books, Inc. 2024
First published in the UK by Penguin Michael Joseph 2025

001

Copyright © Lee Onhwa, 2024
English translation copyright © Slin Jung, 2025

Interior images © Naye, 2024

This book is published with the support of the
Literature Translation Institute of Korea (LTI Korea)

The moral right of the author has been asserted

No part of this book may be used or reproduced in any manner for the purpose of training artificial intelligence technologies or systems. In accordance with Article 4(3) of the DSM Directive 2019/790, Penguin Random House expressly reserves this work from the text and data mining exception

Set in 13.5/17pt Dante MT Std
Typeset by Six Red Marbles UK, Thetford, Norfolk
Printed and bound in Great Britain by Clays Ltd, Elcograf S.p.A.

The authorized representative in the EEA is Penguin Random House Ireland,
Morrison Chambers, 32 Nassau Street, Dublin D02 YH68

A CIP catalogue record for this book is available from the British Library

ISBN: 978–0–241–77685–8

Penguin Random House is committed to a sustainable future
for our business, our readers and our planet. This book is made from
Forest Stewardship Council® certified paper

MIX
Paper | Supporting
responsible forestry
FSC® C018179

CONTENTS

1. Open for Business — 1
2. The First Customer and the Chocolate Jeonbyeong Crackers — 15
3. The Second Customer and the Plum-Blossom Manju Buns — 59
4. The Third Customer and the Green Tea Dango — 131
5. The Fourth Customer and the Strawberry Chapssal-tteok — 185
6. Sa-wol's Story, and the Chestnut Yanggaeng of Goodbye — 227
7. Epilogue — 273

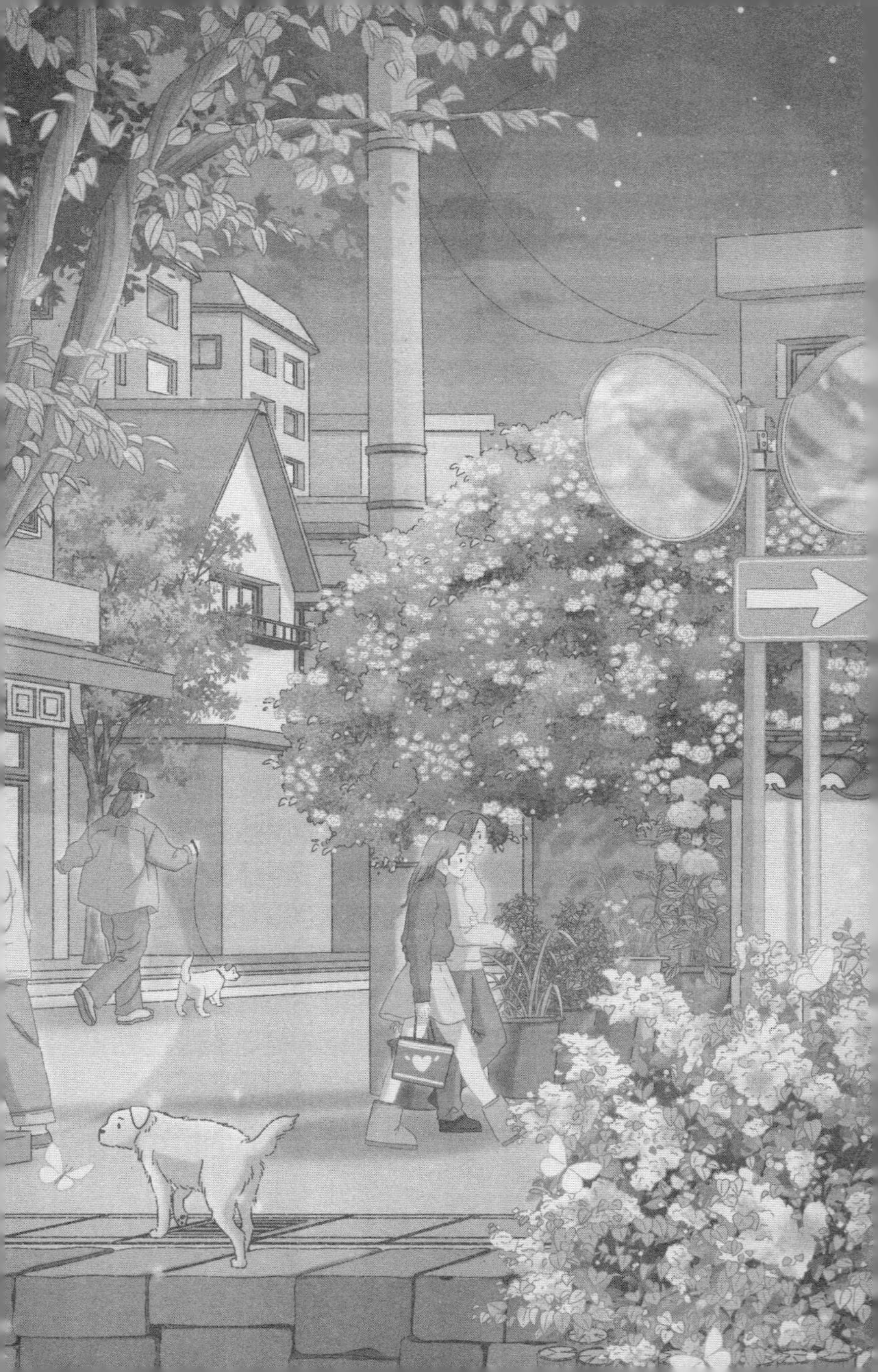

I

Open for Business

Life is a fleeting moment, but our bonds will last forever.
Those were Grandma's last words.

The sky was bright and clear when she left on her final journey, like even death had put on a cloak of sunshine in honour of her gentle humility. It was a lovely spring day with the flowers in spectacular bloom.

I didn't cry.

Grandma's passing didn't destroy my life. I was twenty-seven years old; I could eat, go shopping, and even change the batteries of a dead clock all by myself. I put on a brave face, and life went on as if nothing had happened. I'd known since I was little that even as people died around me, yesterday would still lead into today, which would lead into tomorrow.

She'd closed her eyes with hands folded as neatly

as the life she'd lived. Everything about Grandma's life had been so tidy that it was easy to clean the traces she'd left behind.

'How are you doing these days, Yeon-hwa?'

'I'm all right. I think I'm getting over it now.'

'You keep saying that,' Yi-ryeong said, holding out a wet wipe amidst the packed furniture, 'and that makes me even more worried.'

The truth was, I really *wasn't* holding back tears, or anything like that. The tears just never came – but not because I wasn't sad. Grandma's death *had* hit me out of nowhere, and I'd been devastated. Only not to the point of crying. I think I was just used to saying goodbye since my parents had died in a car crash.

Growing up so resilient wasn't always such a good thing, though.

'Anyway,' I said, changing the subject. 'You know what moving day means? I'm buying us jjajangmyeon noodles!'

'All right!'

'What do you want on the side? Tangsuyuk? Kkanpunggi?'

'Mm, can we splurge a bit and go for whatever's more expensive?'

'Fine, just this once!'

I was pretty sure I deserved to spoil myself: after all, I was filling up a space of my own for the first time in my life! I'd always felt bad about getting tangsuyuk when Grandma was alive, but this time, I was going to reach even higher and order the kkanpunggi. This was the start of a brand-new chapter of my life, and I wouldn't settle for anything less than an upbeat beginning. I could do this!

It was a slow weekday afternoon, so Korean-style Chinese food was the perfect choice. In less than half an hour, Yi-ryeong was throwing open the door with a smile on her face, bringing in a platter of spicy-sweet fried chicken kkanpunggi and two bowls of fresh jjajangmyeon noodles topped with glistening black bean sauce. We coated sauce onto each yellow noodle strand as the pleasant odour of grease filled our nostrils, and our eyes feasted on the fried eggs on top, crispy edges and all. But our jjajangmyeon wasn't complete – not until I sprinkled chilli powder and sesame seeds on top. When I held out the chilli and sesame shakers over Yi-ryeong's bowl, she gulped. I paused with a playful grin.

'Hurry up, Yeon-hwa! I'm starving.'

'You didn't say the magic word.'

'*Please* hurry the hell up, Yeon-hwa. I'm starving.'

I giggled and replied, 'All right, let's dig in!'

We threw ourselves into our meal, almost getting the tips of our noses dirty, and for a while, all we heard was the sound of slurping noodles. The fresh jjajangmyeon was so satisfying that we even forgot to comment, *We should order from here again, they're really good*, and every sweet bite of kkanpunggi only highlighted the flavours of both.

I enjoyed moments like this to the fullest. What did I care if I gained weight or if I went over budget for the month? I wanted to keep on marching forward without worries, without sinking into grief or sadness.

When Yi-ryeong finally looked up from her bowl, she asked, 'What're you going to do about the Hwawoldang?'

'I don't know. I'm going to see Grandma's lawyer about her assets tomorrow,' I replied.

'You don't want to take over after her?' Yi-ryeong wondered. 'You learned a lot about traditional sweets from watching her, right?'

'*Me*, run a business? No way; I'm going to study and get a steady government job. I bet Grandma's holding a well-wishing ritual up there with my parents for my next job interview.'

The Hwawoldang was a traditional sweetshop that had been passed down from my great-great grandmother to her daughter, and then to her daughter after her, each generation changing only the décor and not the recipes. Mum had been next in line, but because she died when I was ten, Grandma had kept it running on her own.

For the next three years or so, I'd spent a lot of time with Grandma at the Hwawoldang after school. But I almost never visited after I'd finished elementary school – meaning that I barely knew a thing about what the shop had become since then. I barely knew my own *neighbours*; family businesses felt like something out of another time period.

Grandma didn't help matters, because she'd always say, *Yeon-hwa, I want you to live a good life.* What was a good life, anyway? The answer was easy: get a good job and live comfortably. The old customer base was disappearing in droves because the shabby apartment buildings around the Hwawoldang were being demolished one after another, and people never looked twice at traditional sweets anyway. Macarons and madeleines were the go-to treats now, and the poor old Hwawoldang might as well have sold chopped liver.

'The regulars'll be sad to see the place go,' Yi-ryeong said as she munched on a crunchy pickled radish.

'What regulars? Grandma was a night owl. She mostly opened up shop at night – I don't know how she thought that would help keep the business afloat.'

'But that sounds really cool! Like *Midnight Diner*.'

'At least the Midnight Diner got customers,' I said sullenly.

'So why *did* she open so late?'

The Grandma I remembered was always working on one traditional sweet or another late into the night, so she wouldn't ever wake up before lunchtime, and I would make and eat breakfast alone. We didn't have much time to sit down for a good talk. She never explained why she opened up shop so late, or why she did any of her work. All I knew was that when the sun went down, Grandma would slather soy sauce onto balls of dango, or dye glutinous rice dough in five different colours.

Her silence made me uncomfortable, and I tried to distance myself from her. I even swallowed my questions because I was afraid she'd think I was a nuisance.

'So even you don't know much about her work?'

'No. Not really,' I admitted.

'Then this is your chance to learn about your grandma,' Yi-ryeong proposed.

I shook my head with a faint smile. Getting to know someone was great, but normally, the people you tried to get to know were *alive*.

But Yi-ryeong seemed to have read my mind, because she said, 'You know, they say memories are *supposed* to appear when there's empty space for them to fill.'

'Is that right?' I replied, and wondered if filling the gaps Grandma had left in my life could help me move forward. I wanted to live without regrets, without a hint of grief about her death – and commemorating her properly was the best way to do that. Cleaning up the Hwawoldang would be the perfect way for me to remember her life and uncover the person she'd been.

I knew what I had to do.

'All right, you've convinced me!' I exclaimed. 'Why not? I'll give this a shot!'

Yi-ryeong beamed, and I knew that I wasn't alone. I could do this. I just knew I could. With hands clenched into determined fists, I sensed the warmth of her friendship gently pushing me onward.

❦

Grandma's lawyer was a man who seemed to be in his fifties and ran a small firm near the Hwawoldang. And although it was a weekday evening, his dark blue suit was as impeccable as though he'd just shown up to the office, and his brows had been trimmed to perfection. The very picture of a reliable professional. He looked over the documents I'd brought before bringing out a bundle of files from his safe.

'You have my sincerest condolences for your loss, Miss Hong,' he said, and held out a paper cup brimming with instant coffee, alongside his business card. 'Now, let me explain to you about the assets Mrs Lim Yun-ok willed to you.'

The coffee was surprisingly good. The water and powder struck a perfect balance that brought me back for another sip, then another. Then I nodded politely and replied, 'I was hoping to liquidate the shop immediately.'

'Yes, I understand,' said the lawyer. 'Mrs Lim's debts were considerable.'

I almost spat my coffee back into the cup.

Grandma had *debts?* Paying off outstanding loans was *not* the reason I'd wanted to liquidate the assets.

The lawyer went on, 'Mrs Lim took out loans to cover the operating costs of her business, which has not turned any profits since its opening. From your reaction, I suppose you were never made aware.'

'H-how much are we talking about here?'

'One hundred million won.'

'What?'

'One hundred million won.'

Grandma, are you serious? One hundred million? That was a decade's worth of rent in Seoul! I gave a hollow laugh and wondered what had possessed Grandma to go that deep into debt for a business that made no money. *Get a hold of yourself, Hong Yeon-hwa! You have to figure out your options* now *before the interest snowballs!*

'That . . . that's a lot,' I managed to say, and asked the key question: 'Um . . . liquidating the business will cover that, right?'

'I'm afraid that no estate agent worth their salt will take the Hwawoldang.'

'Wh-why not?'

'The inauspicious location,' the lawyer said flatly.

'Which happens to be why the area is composed entirely of businesses, and not residences. The whole neighbourhood knows that monks and shamans are regulars there, which means no one will buy for anything more than peanuts.'

Gods, WHY? I'm just a young woman who's been thrown into independence for the first time in her life!

When the lawyer noticed that the cup had crumpled in my hand, he said, 'Miss Hong, your grandmother was aware of the unfortunate circumstances she would leave behind.' He then produced a new document. 'She wrote you this letter, with instructions that will help you address your concerns.'

Dear Yeon-hwa,

By the time you read this letter, I suppose I won't be there to help you.

First, I want to apologize to you for leaving without having explained everything you need to know. But not to worry; I've left behind everything you need at the Hwawoldang, including a way to pay off the debts I've incurred – on three conditions:

1. Personally run the Hwawoldang for at least one month after receiving this letter.
2. Open the shop from ten in the evening to midnight on each business day.
3. Wait in anticipation.

The letter had come straight out of an escape room. The lawyer explained that the ownership of the shop and its rights could be transferred immediately to me, but that the way to repay the debts would be transferred to me by a third party once I'd met her proposed conditions. If I failed, whatever asset it was she had promised would be donated to the needy in accordance with her will.

Wait, wouldn't that put me instantly into impossible debt? Grandma, what is this? What did I do to deserve all this? What am I, a sworn enemy? I was never patient enough to hold my questions – which was partly why I could never get close to Grandma, who took her sweet time doing anything and everything. And now, she'd left behind a slow problem that would demand every ounce of patience I could muster.

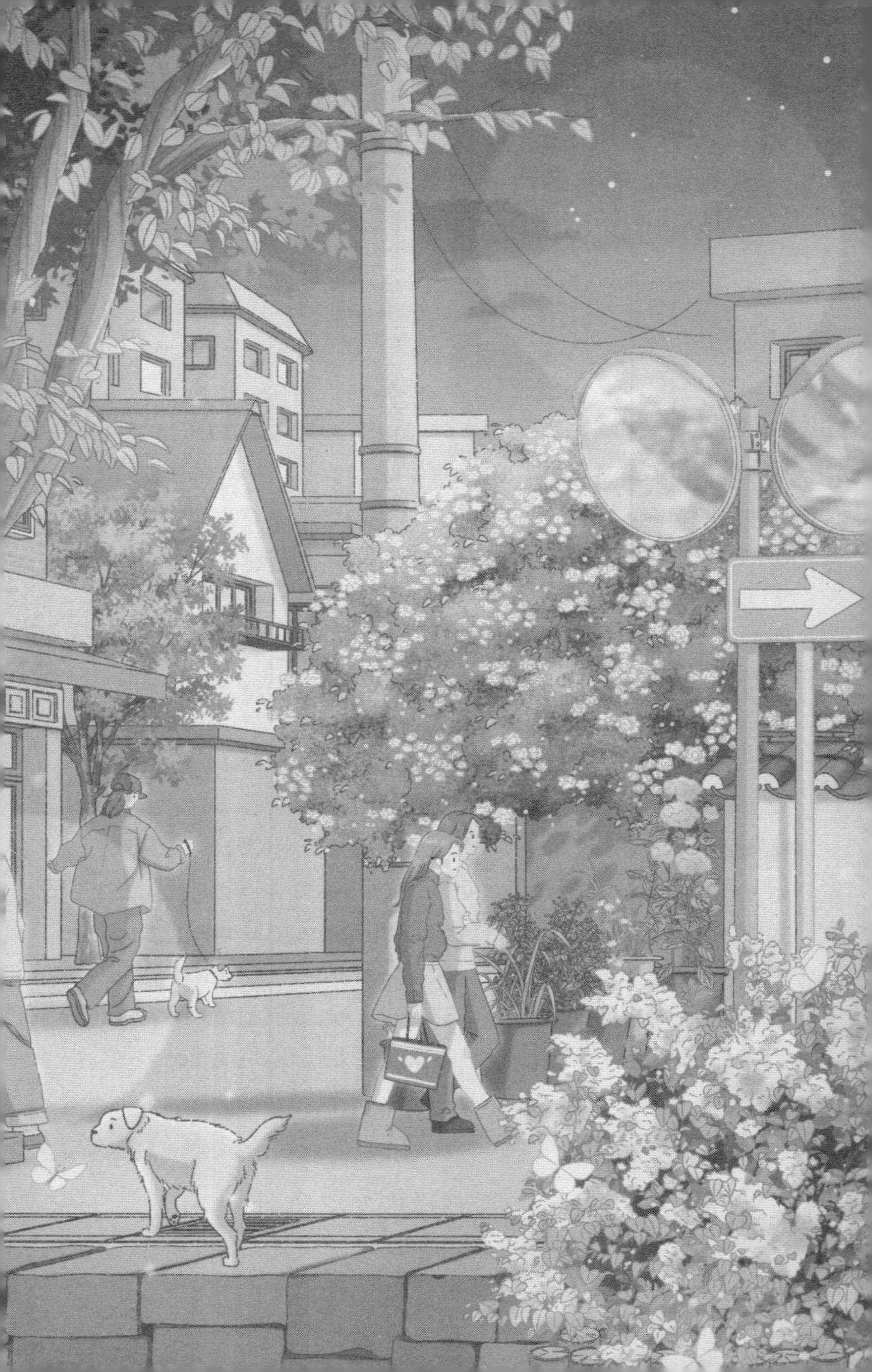

2

The First Customer and the Chocolate Jeonbyeong Crackers

Most people were snug in bed, eyes shut and resting for a busy tomorrow.

I was standing outside the Hwawoldang, its pink neon sign a shock of cherry blossoms in the deep of night.

Once a small, single-storey residence, the traditional sweetshop was packed with décor in bright primary colours, the sort of place that might tempt East Asian versions of Hansel and Gretel. The Chinese characters for 'parting' and 'blessing' were proudly displayed on the wall, below which was an image of a magnificent dragon in flight. The shop interior looked like one massive talisman.

I'd been away for so long that I felt like a stranger. Grandma had never been good at explaining. She'd been the kind of elder you'd want as a friend, but not as family. Ever since I'd been brought into her care, she seemed to avoid spending too much time with me. I hadn't *wanted* to be so quiet around her, but I was afraid she wouldn't like it if I made any trouble. I'd forced myself to be a good grandchild, and being in the shop Grandma had run reminded me of that uncomfortable life.

'I'll liquidate the business as soon as the debt's settled,' I resolved, and stepped forward.

A stainless metal bowl sat outside the entrance, filled with leaves from the tree in front of the building and caked with dirt that seemed to have come from all across the world. The bowl probably belonged to some stray. And it was the first thing I would restore to proper use.

'Meow.'

As I put the clean bowl back in its place, a black cat emerged from an alley in the distance, its bright yellow eyes perfectly clean and its fur shimmering under the sign. It groomed itself, as though nostalgic for someone's touch.

❦

With deliberate steps, I crossed the squeaking tiles and reached the counter, where I found a booklet.

Hwawoldang Recipe No. 1: Jeonbyeong Crackers

I was fond of baking. At the start of the school year, I'd make a big batch of cookies to impress my new classmates and make friends. Making Asian sweets wouldn't be too different, but could I match Grandma's *quality*?

Also known as 'senbei' crackers, these snacks had been brought into Korea during the Japanese occupation and were now loved across the continent. I was supposed to flatten flour dough, cut them into circles, and fry them until their edges were crispy. A sprinkling of powdered green laver would add a hint of saltiness to the flavour, but I didn't like the stuff. *I could try mixing up the recipe, maybe switch the laver for –*

The door chime sang.

'Ah, you're finally open.'

I couldn't believe it. A customer, less than thirty minutes after I turned on the lights? I rushed to put on my apron and stepped forward, trying to explain that I had nothing in stock yet.

'I'm really sorry, but we're still prepping for business. If you could drop in later—'

'So it's true what she said about you taking over.'

I didn't recognize the complete stranger who seemed to know me. He had unusually slender limbs, and when he brushed back his hair, which nearly reached his shoulders, I spotted his fair round brow. His eyes were long and almost snakelike, but not in a bad way.

'You should've dusted the place as soon as you got here. This corner here, it's like it *attracts* dirt,' he said, running a finger across the mother-of-pearl cabinet in the right-hand corner. When he held out the finger and gave an affable smile, I noticed his long eyelashes.

Then I remembered that I was running a *business*, and not wanting to discomfort someone who *had* to be one of Grandma's regulars, I got a wet wipe for the layer of dust on his fingertip. 'I'm so sorry,' I said, 'but who are you?'

'The name's Sa-wol, and I was a supplier for your grandmother,' he said, and added, 'I'm the one you have to bribe.'

'What?'

'I'm kidding.'

The man whose name meant 'April' gave a bark of laughter and held out a box of ingredients and utensils. I wondered why someone my age would willingly work so late in the evening. *Now I'm feeling guilty.*

'You can make the payment in bulk at the end of each month,' Sa-wol said informatively. 'And no,

I don't haggle, give discounts, or run buy-one-get-one-free deals. Sound good to you?'

'I never asked.'

'Means you can't bargain with me,' Sa-wol said with another friendly laugh. Who *guffawed* this late in the evening, anyway? I could practically see down his throat as he laughed at his own joke, and the way he kept pushing back his hair with both hands fully open made him look like a bad theatre actor.

'All right, I get your point,' I finally said. 'I'll collect all your receipts and make the payment in full at the end of the month.'

'Did your grandmother tell you how the shop works?' Sa-wol asked.

'N-no, she never . . .'

'So you really *don't* know who I am?'

'A supplier, right?'

Sa-wol leaned in close, his soft hair almost touching my cheeks. I leaned away in surprise.

Shrugging, he went on, 'You *are* Hong Yeon-hwa, right?'

'How do you know my name?'

'Because *of course* I do. Now, make sure that you don't give away any of the ingredients I bring you. They're *special*, all right?'

Then the door chime sang again, and this time, a middle-aged woman in a flower-print dress entered. I could tell instantly from the nervous look in her eye and her awkward steps that she *had* to be a customer.

Sa-wol noticed the customer, too, and whispered, 'I'm actually a shaman. And I know about the thing your grandmother mentioned in her will. The answer to your "little" problem.'

'You do?' I said in disbelief, but instead of replying, Sa-wol grinned obliviously and turned on his heel. He was out the door before I could ask for an explanation, and gave me a waggle of the brows and a wink as he took one last look into the shopfront.

What in the world was that? I wondered, glaring into the back of his head. But I quickly remembered the customer and put a smile on my face.

The woman came up to the counter and asked, 'Is this the Hwawoldang?'

'Yes, ma'am. But I'm afraid I don't have anything ready for sale yet –'

'But it's half past ten. I don't have time.'

'You could always try tomorrow –'

'No, it *has* to be today. Please,' the woman insisted. 'I'd like some jeonbyeong crackers.'

I gaped. How was I supposed to turn down someone so obviously desperate? *So this is what small businesses struggle with all the time. Weird suppliers and entitled customers.*

'Don't you know what this place does?' the woman finally asked, tilting her head dubiously. She sounded like she knew just as much about the shop as everyone but the person who ran it. With a sigh, she held out her hand. 'There's no time. Take my hand.'

'Wh-what?'

'I'll show you what happened,' the woman said, her eyes reminding me distinctly of a cow being sent to the slaughterhouse.

I couldn't say no to her gaze.

'I was forty-seven years old. My name was Oh Hui-suk.'

Her hands were cold. Too cold. And as I wondered why she spoke in the past tense, the hairs on my skin stood on end and I felt utterly numb.

The Hwawoldang really was now open for business.

❀

Forty-seven-year-old Oh Hui-suk, a supermarket cashier, found it uncomfortable to bend her index finger. She'd had a habit of repeatedly mashing the buttons on the till to get it to work faster, and had put too much stress on her joint. So she bought a plaster and wrapped it around the last joint of the offending digit.

'I feel better already,' she said to herself, taking her usual place behind the register and stretching out her fingers. This was barely an ache, and she knew she wouldn't have to worry too much.

But how was she supposed to handle the *other* source of pain?

'Hui-suk, you can go home a couple of hours early today.'

'No, it's all right. I can keep working.'

'Don't worry, I'll make sure to pay you for those hours.'

'B-but why?'

'Hey, kids' birthdays are important.'

Hui-suk's daughter Ju-yeon turned twenty-seven on that fine spring day, and the manager had worked with Hui-suk for long enough to know about the birthday – and about Hui-suk's dedication to her work over the years. She usually never took days off, opting for compensation at the end of the year instead. A paid holiday was a dream come true.

'I don't remember the last time you took a holiday,' remarked her colleague Se-hui from the next lane. 'You look so happy.'

'Well, it *is* my baby's birthday.'

'Would've thought *you* were the birthday girl, grinning like that. You're *spending* money today, not making it, you know!'

'I know, silly me!' Hui-suk shot back with a giggle. The minutes before opening were always the tensest of the day, but she felt light as a feather, and wouldn't mind no matter how many customers showed up that day with a complicated bundle of coupons.

She'd never known just what Ju-yeon would mean to her, not even on the day she gave birth to the girl. Hui-suk had only been twenty at the time, and her husband much too immature. She was twenty-seven years old when she divorced the man-child, the same age Ju-yeon was now.

Ju-yeon was now a source of immeasurable pain to Hui-suk, but not because she'd had a troubled childhood. In fact, Ju-yeon was mature for her years and a source of constant support. But that only hurt Hui-suk more. She looked down at her finger, each time reminded of the daughter who gave her both joy and heartache.

'What did you get for her present?'

'Oh, she doesn't really like presents.'

'Who *doesn't* like presents? You can't just go empty-handed.'

'Don't worry, I have a little something for Ju-yeon.'

'Like what?'

'Her favourite snack,' Hui-suk said, but fingered the white envelope she'd slipped into her pocket – the *real* present she made a point of not mentioning. 'By the way, Se-hui. Are you going to be busy next spring?'

'How am I supposed to know? I guess I'll still be here, cashing out customers.'

'Do you think you could spare one day in the weekend?'

'For what?'

'Wedding bells.'

Se-hui clapped a hand to her mouth, stifling an excited squeal. Her free hand waved uncontrollably in furious congratulations. 'Oh my gosh!' she finally managed. 'I'm so happy for you, Hui-suk!'

Se-hui's excitement was contagious. Before she knew it, Hui-suk was scrolling through her phone, searching for a picture of her future son-in-law, but as if on cue, a crowd of customers reached the registers. The two cashiers smiled awkwardly as they went back to work.

Hui-suk knew that Ju-yeon deserved so much more than she'd got. She wished she could have bought the girl a set of expensive clothes, or a brand-name bag – but Ju-yeon showed her nothing but gratitude, which made Hui-suk both happy and guilty that her daughter had grown up so well despite the loneliness of her childhood.

But today, she would make things right, if only by a little. All the money she'd saved by refusing holidays had been withdrawn in cash and placed neatly inside the envelope now in her pocket. *I'm so glad I can still do something for her*, she thought, and at the end of her shift, picked up a package of laver-sprinkled jeonbyeong crackers from the snack corner.

❀

Hui-suk couldn't remember the last time she'd walked home while the sun was up. With the bag of green laver jeonbyeong crackers under one arm, she let herself take in the sky for once. It had been twenty-seven springs since Ju-yeon was born, and not once had it rained on her birthday.

It's like even the sky wants to celebrate my precious

girl, she thought, knowing what a blessing it was to be happy without having much to her name. She headed home with a spring in her step and gratitude even for the most mundane of details. At home, she rushed to the kitchen. She had to finish dinner preparations before Ju-yeon came back from work. As much as she loved her daughter, Hui-suk was never good at expressing herself. Just thinking about saying the words *I love you* or *thank you* made her red with embarrassment. All she could do was express those feelings with her actions, and with a generous helping of beef in the miyeokguk soup.

'Mum? You're home early today,' Ju-yeon exclaimed as she walked into the house.

Hui-suk replied, 'I am, aren't I? Now go wash up so we can have dinner.'

The miyeokguk soup – the traditional birthday dish – came rising to a simmer as Ju-yeon showered, and Hui-suk busied herself plating the sides and setting the table. Finally, she arranged several laver jeonbyeong on a wooden plate.

Ju-yeon sniffed the air happily as she emerged from the bathroom, drawn by the savoury smell. 'Thanks, Mum.'

'Eat up, Birthday Girl,' Hui-suk insisted. She'd

grilled up ham and crispy beef yukjeon slices, whirled together japchae noodles with a generous sprinkling of sesame seeds, and steamed rice with expensive red beans from the markets that the merchant had refused to let her haggle for. Everything on the table was a luxury, even if it seemed like an ordinary old-school party meal. Hui-suk had packed each dish with love and effort.

In their family, love was always expressed through flavour, not words.

'Laver jeonbyeong, too!' Ju-yeon said, noticing the wooden plate. 'That takes me back.'

'Your dessert,' Hui-suk said, pushing the plate in her direction. Ju-yeon nodded brightly in place of an answer, still chewing.

When she was little, Ju-yeon hated the fact her mother worked so late. But she'd never shown it, because complaining would only make things harder for her mother. Still, she wished her mother could spend a little more time with her – and so, Ju-yeon had recorded Hui-suk's favourite TV shows ahead of time and mopped the part of the floor where she usually sat.

Hui-suk would always come home from work to the same sight: the TV playing her favourite funny show and the conspicuously shiny spot on the floor with the best view of the screen. But that wasn't what showed her just how much Ju-yeon missed her each day. Hui-suk could tell how lonesome she was from the way the girl rushed to the door. When she desperately held back the words 'I'm so happy you're home', Ju-yeon had thought she'd fooled her mother, but her naïve determination turned to maturity – and it had happened so fast that Hui-suk felt guilty.

But there *was* one thing Ju-yeon allowed herself to ask for:

Could you please pick up some snacks on the way home?

When she arrived at work, Hui-suk had realized that she had no idea what snacks Ju-yeon liked. She knew that most snacks were sweet or salty, but couldn't decide on which – until she spotted the jeonbyeong crackers with the laver sprinkles. The edges were sweet, and the centre salty.

I hope she likes it, she thought, hesitantly handing Ju-yeon the bag of jeonbyeong. To her relief, Ju-yeon jumped for joy, sitting in the living room with the cylindrical package between her knees, munching on one cracker after another.

Afterwards, Hui-suk picked up laver jeonbyeong regularly on her way home – the very same brand each time, which put the very same smile on Ju-yeon's face.

Hui-suk roused herself from her memories and took another spoonful of seaweed soup, savouring the extra layer of umami, and announced: 'I have something for you.'

'Ooh, a birthday present?'

'It's not much, but I hope it helps,' Hui-suk replied, holding out an envelope with crumpled corners. Ju-yeon waved her hands politely to refuse when she realized what must be inside, but Hui-suk held it out insistently. 'It's yours.'

'But you worked so hard to make that money.'

'I was working so hard for *you*.'

Ju-yeon hadn't wanted to burden her mother with the wedding. She didn't want pomp and fanfare anyway, so she hadn't said a word about the costs. But she couldn't bring herself to turn down her mother's offer of love, held together in this little envelope of cash. Thankful and guilty all at once, Ju-yeon dabbed at her eyes and hung her head. 'Thank you, Mum. I'll be frugal with it, I promise.'

'Use it like water,' Hui-suk said, not showing her emotions. She dipped her spoon deep into her soup and brought up seaweed. It tasted just as salty as the laver, and she could almost feel the same saltiness in her eyes. An unfamiliar feeling that seemed to clear the exhaustion from her life.

That night, mother and daughter sat in front of the TV, watching dramas as they snacked on even more jeonbyeong crackers. Ju-yeon had a habit of eating the edges first, saving the salty centres to eat at the end. Hui-suk was reminded of the way Ju-yeon used to save up her pocket money. Once, they'd had a conversation like this:

'Mum, I'm gonna buy new socks with my allowance.'

'But we have so many socks at home. Save your money for something else.'

'But I saw these really cute ones in the shop.'

'No one can see your socks once you put on your shoes. It's best to keep your money for really important things.'

Hui-suk had taught her daughter not to waste her money on frivolous things, and Ju-yeon grew up to be a frugal young woman – she even made sure to put away savings every month. As a mother, she'd always wanted to give Ju-yeon more, but decided to look on the bright side: thanks to her upbringing, Ju-yeon had learned to manage her money wisely.

Was that also why she always saved the laver-sprinkled centres to the end?

Hui-suk stared curiously at Ju-yeon as the latter munched away, distinctly feeling as though her daughter was a little girl again.

'Something on my face, Mum?'

'No, I just thought you didn't need to hoard the centre pieces anymore.'

'Oh, the crackers?'

'Exactly. I can buy you more if you want, no need to save those bits.'

'Heh, where did that come from? It's okay, Mum.'

They chatted in front of the TV until late into the night. Hui-suk would always be grateful for these moments, but she simply couldn't help the sadness of knowing that soon her darling Ju-yeon was going to move out and start a new life. The living room would feel so much emptier, and her eyes stung. Hui-suk playfully snatched one of the centre pieces Ju-yeon had saved and popped it into her mouth. 'I can't wait to see you leave,' she said, crunching. 'Then I can have all these jeonbyeong to myself.'

Ju-yeon could tell her mother was lying. She was the world's only translator for her mother's own brand of language. 'I'll drop in all the time, Mum.'

'No one invited you, dear.'

'But I'll miss you.'

'You're not supposed to spend too much time with your mother once you're married. Stick to Gi-hun like glue.'

'Yeah, right.'

'I'm being serious here, Ju-yeon.'

'And I know you don't really mean what you said.'

As the last of the jeonbyeong melted away in her mouth, Hui-suk seared the flavour into her memories. Meanwhile, Ju-yeon went to her room and emerged with a paper bag printed with the logo of an expensive department store.

'And I know what you'll say when you see what's inside,' Ju-yeon said, and pushed the bag into Hui-suk's hands.

Hui-suk reached into the bag and felt something soft and lightweight.

Ju-yeon went on, 'Thank you for everything, Mum.'

When she pulled the object into view, Hui-suk's jaw dropped. The dress was white silk, and decorated with bright yellow hydrangeas. 'What is this, Ju-yeon?'

'A present. You should wear it for the family picture next time.'

'But today is *your* birthday, not mine.'

'Yeah, but this is my last birthday at home,' Ju-yeon replied. 'I wanted to make sure you know how much I appreciate you.' Then she sank into the sofa and awkwardly fiddled with the remote.

Hui-suk, for her part, could only go on asking why Ju-yeon would buy her something like this, all the while studying the lovely dress up and down. She didn't know when her daughter had gone from a child to such a considerate young woman; when she'd learned to make her mother cry tears of joy. She tried to quickly hide her emotions with a sleeve across her eyes, but she didn't have quite enough sleeve to conceal the feelings that brimmed in her heart.

'Oh, Mum,' Ju-yeon whispered gently, hugging her mother from behind, 'deep down, you're such a softie.'

Unable to wipe her tears or open up the folded dress again, Hui-suk stood in a storm of emotions. She wanted to show just how thankful she was, but all she could do was stare out at the warm darkness outside the window.

The laver-powdered jeonbyeong pieces still lay on the plate, growing moist under her tears.

Around noon that weekend, Hui-suk emerged from the kitchen in the midst of cooking somyeon noodles to find Ju-yeon with a shopping bag of expensive stationery paper, envelopes and stickers.

'What's all this for, Ju-yeon?'

'Wedding invitations,' Ju-yeon replied, looking up. She explained that the invitations would be handmade, and that she'd make half a dozen for practice before Gi-hun arrived to help out and join them for lunch.

Hui-suk was in disbelief. 'Who makes their own invitations in this day and age? Can't you just have them ordered?'

'We don't even have fifty guests,' Ju-yeon said. 'That's not nearly enough for the minimum printing.'

'Still, it's so much work,' Hui-suk said, but she was secretly proud of both Ju-yeon and Gi-hun.

Gi-hun was just as sweet and frugal as Ju-yeon, and his family situation wasn't so different from hers, either. He'd thrown himself into the workforce at a young age, and didn't have many friends to invite to the wedding – which the couple seemed to accept as a blessing. A small wedding would cost less time and money. They both saw the silver lining even in circumstances other people saw as misfortunes.

'It's so much to do by hand,' Hui-suk insisted. 'Are you sure you can do this?'

Ju-yeon smiled. 'We have plenty of paper. And plenty of time before we have to hand them out.'

'I just don't want you to tire yourselves trying to pinch every penny,' Hui-suk said. She wished her daughter wouldn't have to work so hard because she couldn't afford anything else.

'Don't say that, Mum,' Ju-yeon replied gently. 'I'm trying to add a personal touch to the process. Gi-hun and I are doing this for ourselves.'

Hui-suk couldn't argue. The smile on Ju-yeon's face was genuine. But her pride in her darling daughter still hurt – and that pain, like the ache in her finger, would always be part of her life.

❀

'Here, let me help – the noodles are going to take a while to cook.'

'Thanks, Mum. I'll write the invitations, so could you put them in the envelopes and seal them?'

Hui-suk listened attentively to Ju-yeon's instructions. Soon, one finished invitation slid into her hands, and she put that into an envelope and sealed it with a red sticker. It looked like a perfect, store-bought package. And the process was surprisingly fun.

'You know what?' Ju-yeon remarked. 'I'm going to become a calligrapher in my next life.'

'Why not this one? You could still do calligraphy for fun after work,' Hui-suk said, but Ju-yeon held up her next half-finished letter.

'Not with this chicken scratch.'

Hui-suk burst into laughter at the squiggles on the beautiful stationery paper.

'What about you, Mum? What do you want to be in your next life?' Ju-yeon asked.

'I like the life I have.'

'Don't you ever want to try something else? Like, running a business? Becoming a movie star?'

'I . . . I don't know.' A singer who'd been a regular guest on their favourite comedy show was performing on TV, belting out his new song as he crisscrossed the stage. 'Hm . . . I think I might want to try being a singer.'

'That's cool. Why?'

'I could sing the most embarrassing things without batting an eye,' Hui-suk replied as the camera zoomed in on the singer, and soon she was seeing herself on the screen, proudly putting her affection for her daughter into words without a shred of embarrassment. But even thinking about it left her scratching her head awkwardly.

'Mum, I think the noodles are boiling.'

Hui-suk leapt to her feet as the pot trembled on the stovetop. 'Oh my goodness! I almost burned the house down.'

She'd found herself forgetting small details more and more these days. Was she just tired from work? Hui-suk hadn't forgotten anything important, but she could tell that she needed a break. She turned down the heat and stirred with a pair of wooden chopsticks. The noodles swam like jellyfish in the pot.

As if on cue, the doorbell rang, and Ju-yeon rushed to the door. Gi-hun announced himself politely and clearly as soon as he was inside, and Hui-suk smiled at the energy behind his voice as she wiped her hands and went to greet him.

'Good afternoon, Mother,' Gi-hun said with a friendly smile, arranging his shoes neatly by the door. Hui-suk had never seen him in anything but clean coats and jackets, never splurging on luxuries but always dressed his best. He had a wide brow and round earlobes, which all made him look just as vivacious and young as Ju-yeon. Hui-suk nodded approvingly at the man who would be her daughter's greatest source of joy.

'Good afternoon, Gi-hun,' she replied. 'Please tell me you're staying for lunch.'

Gi-hun smiled, 'I'd love that, Mother. I brought us dessert to share.'

'I do hope you won't mind doing the dishes, either,' Hui-suk joked, and Gi-hun chuckled as he answered, 'I certainly won't.'

When Gi-hun placed a bulging plastic bag of snacks on the table, Ju-yeon affectionately chided him for buying so much. Hui-suk hoped that Ju-yeon would have a much happier marriage than she had had. Ever since the engagement, she'd been feeling a mix of nostalgia, sadness, happiness and joy at every sight of Ju-yeon. The marriage wouldn't change much about her life, but Hui-suk still felt as if a big chunk of herself was about to be taken away, as if every emotion in the world came rushing together towards her like a wave before it departed again.

The noodles were fully cooked, and smelled so sweet she wanted to cry.

Hui-suk slathered seasoning all over the somyeon noodles to make bibimguksu. She'd gone a little overboard with the seasoning and her tongue cried out for water, but Gi-hun didn't complain once as he polished off his bowl.

Afterwards, the little family sat in a row in the living room to work on the rest of the invitations. Ju-yeon wrote them, Gi-hun put them into the envelopes, and Hui-suk sealed them with stickers, until they had nearly two dozen ready to give away – then Ju-yeon threw herself onto the sofa in exhaustion.

Gi-hun reached into the bag of snacks. 'Want some chocolate-covered biscuits, Ju-yeon?'

'Wait, she doesn't really like those,' Hui-suk said quickly. 'I'll go get the jeonbyeong crackers.'

But Gi-hun gave her a confused look as he opened up the box and said, 'Oh, I didn't know that. Ju-yeon always says that chocolate-covered biscuits are her favourite.' He pulled out a biscuit and put it into Ju-yeon's mouth. She took it with a smile. Hui-suk couldn't believe how happy she looked to eat something she probably had never tried.

What Gi-hun said next, however, surprised her even more.

'Ju-yeon told me that she loves chocolate for dessert.'

'What?'

'She always goes for the chocolate-covered treats when we eat out together, and she goes wild for the candy discounts on White Day. I've never seen her touch the salty stuff.'

Ju-yeon slapped her belly and snickered. 'My mum doesn't really understand me, Gi-hun.'

Something inside Hui-suk seemed to break. She watched Ju-yeon and Gi-hun laugh and chatter over their chocolate-covered biscuits, and then looked bitterly down at her basket of jeonbyeong crackers. *But I thought these were her favourite.* The brown jeonbyeong crackers looked paltry in the plastic bag. *She jumped for joy when I brought them home. She ate every last piece.*

Then she remembered what she'd told young Ju-yeon when she brought the jeonbyeong home:

'These are the cheapest and biggest snacks on the shelf.'

Ju-yeon had been too selfless. Even when she'd asked for snacks, she'd never said *which*. Maybe what she'd really wanted wasn't a treat to snack on, but her mother's love, represented in the act of picking, buying and bringing the jeonbyeong home.

Finally, Hui-suk realized that Ju-yeon had been hiding her emotions and holding back her words just as much as her.

She looked up and saw her darling little girl beaming next to the man she'd chosen, enjoying a pack of the snacks she actually liked. She wondered when the young woman with the radiant smile had stopped being a child and grown into adulthood.

Hui-suk's heart ached.

❀

On a weekday morning several days later, Ju-yeon went out with Gi-hun for wedding preparations. She wouldn't be back until late that day, and Hui-suk saw her chance.

This time, she requested the holiday herself. The supermarket happened to have a large number of cashiers that day, so the manager let her take the day off. So like usual, Hui-suk picked up a pack of jeon-byeong crackers from the shelves – but this time, she dropped by a baking supply shop for cooking chocolate, butter and whipped cream.

'Ma'am,' said the storekeeper, pausing. 'This chocolate is a little harder to melt than the other kind. Would that be all right?'

Hui-suk paused. She didn't know much about baking, let alone the kinds of chocolate in the world. 'D-does this mean this is low quality?'

'Not at all. It's considered higher-end, with a longer-lasting chocolate aroma. You just can't melt it like other kinds of chocolate; make sure to double-boil it on low heat for a long time.'

'But this is the better kind?'

'It is.'

'Then I'll take it.'

The shopkeeper explained again that Hui-suk's chosen chocolate would take longer to melt down than other kinds, but Hui-suk didn't mind. She had all afternoon. Today, she would happily give her daughter what she'd truly wanted all these years, and with the best ingredients.

It was all so simple.

Hui-suk would apologize for everything with a plate of chocolate-covered jeonbyeong crackers. There was no shortage of DIY recipes online. All she had to do was coat the crackers in melted chocolate, adding butter and whipped cream to the mix for an even deeper flavour. Her present would be her way of saying, *I'm sorry I didn't take the time to understand who you really are.*

The second she got home, Hui-suk filled a double-boiling pot partway with water, put it on the stove, put a bowl on top and added the chocolate. Then she arranged oven mitts and a wooden spoon next to the stove. But the chocolate showed no sign of melting anytime soon, just like the shopkeeper had said. Hui-suk didn't want to waste her afternoon, so ironed out the flower-print dress while she waited.

'She even got the flowers in my favourite colour,' she said with a smile, downcast at the fact that Ju-yeon knew her better than she knew Ju-yeon.

Once the dress had been ironed out, Hui-suk daydreamed of their trip to the photography studio. The thought of wearing that dress and standing in front of the camera together with Ju-yeon and Gi-hun made her giggle excitedly in spite of her guilt.

'Maybe I'll watch some YouTube,' she said, noting that the chocolate was still nowhere close to melting. As the scent of cocoa filled the living room, Hui-suk lay on the sofa to rest, playing a ten-minute video her colleagues had recommended. All the exhaustion drained from her body as she laughed along to the clip.

A fresh breeze blew in through the balcony windows, and the chatter of children drifted in from the playground. It was a warm, peaceful day. There were still three minutes left on the video when Hui-suk's eyelids slid shut.

'It's so nice to take a day off once in a while.'

Like candyfloss dipped into a piping-hot bath, she let herself sink into the sofa.

❀

When Hui-suk opened her eyes, her phone was dark.

'What is that smell?'

She sensed heat from the kitchen, and leapt to her feet in horror as she spotted the roaring ball of fire on the countertop.

Her nap was only supposed to be for ten minutes, but Hui-suk had slept for an entire hour. The flames were much too large to blow out, and had spread to the oven mitts and wooden spoon she had so neatly arranged by the stove. The warm, dry breeze from the windows only fanned the fire further, until it was gobbling up everything from the washcloths to the tablecloth, the chairs and the dining table. The faded old appliances began to spark, and soon new fires were sprouting left and right. All hint of sleep evaporated from Hui-suk.

'Oh no, oh no, what do I do?'

Plunged into panic and confusion, Hui-suk found herself closing the windows to stop the wind. She tried to call the fire department, but her hands shook so much that she kept dropping her phone.

In the meantime, the fire spread relentlessly across the kitchen and now threatened the master bedroom and the living room – most importantly, the large fabric sofa she had just slept in. If the fire reached the sofa, it would all be over. Even as her mind told her that she had to pick up her phone from the floor and call the fire department, she tried to put out the fire herself with some clothes and blankets. But nothing she'd seen in the movies would work, and only filled the house with black smoke. Her head hurt.

'I-I have to stay calm! I'll call the fire department and get out of here!'

Knowing that she could do nothing, Hui-suk managed to dial the number, then squeezed her feet into her shoes and opened the door – and went all the way down the corridor, ringing all the doorbells on the way. She realized that tears were running down her face.

'FIRE!' she cried. 'I'm from Unit 402! There's a fire in the house! You have to get out of here, now!'

'What?'

One by one, shocked neighbours emerged from their homes. They grabbed the fire extinguishers, but couldn't get them to work correctly. In the meantime, smoke began to seep from Hui-suk's door.

'Let's all get out of the building first! We can't do anything ourselves.'

Having lost all hope, the neighbours managed to coax Hui-suk downstairs. Soon, the corridors were thick with smoke. Hui-suk had worked herself to the bone to afford the lease on the unit. She wished she'd listened to the estate agent who'd explained that the building was 'a little far from the closest fire station'.

If only I hadn't fallen asleep. If only I'd turned off the stove. Hui-suk couldn't stop blaming herself. But just as she sighed in relief that she had managed to escape with her life, she recalled something horrible.

'The wedding invitations!'

Ju-yeon had taken time out of her busy schedule to work on those invitations. Hui-suk remembered how the three of them had worked together to finish them all, and how the papers would surely burn to ashes. She also remembered the pretty dress. The gift from Ju-yeon, which she'd stupidly left in the burning living room.

'No . . . she worked so hard on those . . .'

She didn't care if the fire devoured the TV they'd painstakingly chosen, the dressers they'd got second-hand, or the massive refrigerator she'd been almost too reluctant to buy. None of those were worth more than her life.

She couldn't say the same for the invitations that Ju-yeon and Gi-hun had made with love.

She needed those bundles of paper. The paper that cost almost nothing to buy, that could be printed by the thousands at the local shop. Wedding invitations were scraps of pulp. But people did foolish things for less. The love that had been poured into those humble invitations drove her mad with terror and worry.

Giving up on those invitations would be like letting Ju-yeon's hard-earned happiness die in the flames, Hui-suk felt. And she couldn't let anything hurt a hair on the poor girl's head.

'Ma'am, where are you going?'

'I just forgot a few things! I'll be out soon!'

The neighbours tried, and failed, to stop her. Hui-suk broke into a run, and although people tried to chase her up the steep staircases, they were soon scared off by the plumes of smoke.

Hui-suk burst into Unit 402, shielding her nose and mouth with a sleeve. The fire was a raging inferno now, and her legs trembled, but thankfully, Ju-yeon's room was close to the front door.

'I just need the invitations . . . just the invitations . . .'

It was the easiest job in the world. All she had to do was retrieve one shopping bag filled with nothing but paper. Hui-suk wove through the flames and entered Ju-yeon's room. The smoke made it hard to see, but she rubbed her stinging eyes and managed to grab the bag.

But as she made her way out, she spotted the dress, still lying on the ironing board.

I forgot!

Fortunately, she hadn't been far. Hui-suk reached the dress with ease and held it close as she turned.

A sharp pain seemed to break her skull to pieces. She choked on the air she breathed, gasping even louder each time and finding only smoke.

Just a few more steps . . .

But she couldn't stop coughing now. Ju-yeon's love, packed into the shopping bag at her side, urged her to fly away. Hui-suk couldn't let her down. She panted. Then she felt something strike the back of her head, and her eyes shut against her will. Her legs trembled as she felt something slide horribly out of her, but she gathered herself and willed her feet forward. The door was so close. She took one step, then another. Her eyes swam and her throat burned. She couldn't think. Each time she coughed, smoke filled her lungs and clouded more of her brain. But she couldn't stop coughing.

She just had to make it out the door. Her humble little abode, where she'd spent half her life, wasn't nearly big enough to take away her love for Ju-yeon.

Hui-suk fell limp anyway.

❀

It took less than an hour for me to see – and emerge from – the stranger's life.

'Do you understand now?' the woman pleaded as I shook off her hand. She looked like a perfectly normal person, so what in the world did I just see? Was it all a dream? Was I really that tired?

But it was all too real. I couldn't put it into words, but I could feel the woman's grief with every inch of myself. Her pain and sorrow were overwhelming.

'They said I could be reincarnated into anything I want, if I can get something from this shop,' the woman explained. 'Today's my last day; I *have* to get a traditional snack here before midnight.'

'*Reincarnate?*' I repeated in disbelief.

The woman replied, 'Yes, *reincarnate*. The Hwawoldang is supposed to comfort the dead before they finally pass, at least according to the person that told me.'

I'd have called her crazy – but the woman had no shadow. She was a ghost, and I had no reason to doubt the dead. Not believing her would be an insult to her memory, after everything I'd seen of her life.

The clock was ticking. I had no time to lose. 'Let me get that chocolate-covered jeonbyeong ready for you.'

'Thank you. Please, I need it before midnight.'

I rushed into the open kitchen and prepared the dough, mixing melted butter with plain flour and fine almond powder. Then I added egg whites to powdered sugar in a separate bowl, then combined both mixtures. I shaped the dough into balls, flattening them out for the crunchy texture that defined jeonbyeong crackers, and placed them into the preheated oven to bake for ten minutes.

'Excuse me, what's that smell?'

Oh no! They're burning!

I kicked myself. I'd flattened the dough so much that ten minutes had been too long. My first batch was covered in cracks, and sweat ran down my brow as if *I'd* been in the oven myself. The clock pointed to half past eleven.

'Don't worry, ma'am!' I said with a reassuring laugh. 'They're turning out a *lovely* golden brown!'

Life sometimes meant you had to tell white lies for the greater good, or something to that effect. I quickly started a new batch, this time making sure the flattened dough *wasn't* as thin as paper, and set the oven timer to eight minutes.

Thankfully, the second time was the charm. The next step was the chocolate coating – where I had to express the dead woman's love for her daughter with the sweetness the daughter had tried to hide her fondness for all her life. If I could only put effort into one thing in my life, this had to be it.

I crushed some chocolate into bits, double-boiled it and melted it down until it was smooth as, well, butter, and brushed a thin layer onto the second batch of golden-brown jeonbyeong. The chocolate went across the whole surface, so that the first bite – wherever that was – would always be packed with the family's love.

Unfortunately, the second batch of jeonbyeong also cracked with a horrible snap. The pressure of the brush had been too heavy.

'There's fifteen minutes left. Is everything all right?'

'Don't worry, ma'am! Desserts are supposed to taste better when you're desperate!'

'I don't think I've heard that one before.'

'Industry secret, ma'am!' I replied with a forced laugh as sweat continued to run down my brow. I quickly rolled out more dough, baked it in the oven, and coated the new batch in chocolate – but this time, I didn't use a brush. I dipped the jeonbyeong into the melted chocolate instead. *This is why we need trial and error.*

I looked down at my watch. It told me it was thirty seconds past 11:58.

She needs this jeonbyeong in ninety seconds! I picked up one cracker and sprinted out the door, but wasted precious seconds when my apron strap got caught on the way. *Come on!* I wriggled myself free and reached the counter.

'It's done! Quickly, take a bite!'

'Just put it into my mouth –'

'Here!'

It was three seconds to midnight when the woman took a bite of the jeonbyeong. There was a pleasant crunch as the thin cracker split clean in two. The tension drained from my body.

'Just in time,' the woman said.

'How does it taste, ma'am? Do you like it?'

Beaming, the woman replied, 'It's so sweet. My daughter will love it.'

With a sigh of relief, I slid the rest of the chocolate-covered jeonbyeong into a long, clean plastic bag and held it out to the woman.

But she wouldn't take it.

'Is something wrong?'

'I got what I wanted,' she replied. 'Please get the rest to my daughter. She has a reddish mole on her index finger. You'll know when you see her.'

I had no idea where the woman's daughter was or what she was doing. And I couldn't exactly up and leave to go find her.

But before I could refuse, I heard a meow.

The black cat from earlier appeared at the door.

The woman opened the door for it, and it slipped behind the counter and batted the bag of jeonbyeong from my hand.

'Wait! You'll get sick if you eat that!' I cried.

The cat, though, didn't try to open the bag. Instead, it went up to the woman, who spread her arms to welcome it. The cat gently thumped its head into the woman's stomach.

'She says she'll take these to my daughter,' the woman said brightly.

'This *cat*?'

'My daughter's going to have a dream,' the woman explained, 'of eating these jeonbyeong with me. I saw it when this cat bumped into me.' Then she gave the cat an affectionate pat on her little head. 'Tell her I loved her very much, little one. Tell her how much I cared, and how much I want to apologize.'

The cat's golden eyes seemed to glimmer as she slipped out the door, still carrying the jeonbyeong in her mouth. She vanished so quickly that I thought the bell around her neck must be magical, like a key into the woman's daughter's dreams.

'The jeonbyeong was so good that it makes the years I lived seem just as sweet,' the woman finally said.

'I'm glad to hear that.'

'But I need to apologize,' the woman added.

'For what?'

'I'm afraid a ghost like me can't pay you for your work. I can give you something else —'

What? This is a dine-and-dash! I couldn't bring myself to say so, though. I wanted to respect the dead, even if they made weird, rushed requests in the middle of the night. The woman who'd once been a mum, a supermarket cashier, and a person who loved the people in her life, was now pale as a sheet. Too pale to be among the living.

Midnight had been and gone. I wished I could give this spirit a little more time, but the woman went to the glass door. She looked like a weight had been lifted from her shoulders.

'Are you heading out already?' I asked.

'Yes. My business is done.'

'Don't you have any other regrets?'

The woman smiled. 'Absolutely none. I'm satisfied with what I had. I only hope that in my next life, I'll be able to sing, in whatever form I take.'

'I'm surprised. People aren't usually this accepting of death.'

'I suppose not. But I know why I'm looking forward to what happens next.'

'And why is that?'

'Dead men tell no tales,' she replied playfully.

The door chime sang yet again, and suddenly only a gust of wind remained where the woman once stood. Specks of light glimmered in the air, and the scent of hydrangeas seemed to ride on the breeze, like a stroll through a lush garden in midnight.

I remembered the sweetness of the chocolate jeonbyeong – the flavour that gave the woman a final taste of comfort – as I waved goodbye to her absence.

I went back to the counter and saw a neatly folded dress lying there. It was patterned with bright yellow hydrangeas.

3

The Second Customer and the Plum-Blossom Manju Buns

The next day, I went to the Hwawoldang a little before opening time.

If I'd heard the first customer right, the door of the shop was like a boundary between life and death. Grandma had spent all those nights sending off the dead to the world beyond. My heart pounded when I thought about my new role. Could I really help the dead with their final requests? Making traditional sweets was hard enough without the pressure of fulfilling dying wishes on top. I was so nervous that I stayed up all night after that encounter, like I'd downed three cups of coffee in a row.

Did the dead really get reincarnated? And would the black cat really visit the woman's daughter's dreams and deliver those chocolate-covered jeon-byeong? I hoped it was all true. Half-anxious and half-excited, I decided to master all of Grandma's old recipes.

'Excuse me, do you sell red chestnut yanggaeng jelly?'

The man in the tidy business suit showed up just as I was measuring out ingredients. *Did he die at the office?* He looked so perfectly healthy I wanted to cry. My eyebrows rose as I went up to him.

'Welcome. I'm so sorry, you must have had a long trip.'

'What?'

'It's all right, I understand. And you look as healthy as if you were still alive, if I might say so.'

'Healthy? I have really bad gastritis.'

I took his hand gently in mine. He was so warm for a disembodied spirit.

'Excuse me, what are you doing?' the man questioned.

I finally noticed the look of confusion and irritation on his face and let go. 'Wait . . . are you . . . human?' I asked, stepping back.

'Do I look like a chimpanzee to you?'

'So . . . um . . . you're not . . . dead?'

'*Dead?* What are you talking about? I just wanted some red chestnut yanggaeng jelly,' the man said with a frown. 'Never mind.' He hauled open the door and walked out without another word as I stood frozen in shock.

So the shop gets live customers too, I realized, and rushed behind the counter in shame to bury my nose in the recipe booklet.

Two hours of measuring practice later, the door opened again.

'Feeling a bit more motivated now, are we?'

Sa-wol. Today, he'd tied his hair into a neat ponytail, and was dressed in a jade-coloured modernized hanbok. The getup would have looked silly on anyone else, but he had the long legs and neck to gracefully pull off the Goryeo celadon look.

'Do you have more supplies for me?' I asked.

Sa-wol grinned. 'No, yesterday's batch should cover you for a while,' he said, and strutted around the floor, scanning the walls and running his fingers over surfaces for dust to blow away. He even deigned to adjust the crooked fixtures and decorations.

I still had no idea what exactly he was supposed to be – a supplier and a shaman, apparently – and although he didn't say out loud, he knew Grandma and the Hwawoldang's secret.

'So,' I said, 'are you alive?'

'I'm a young and handsome shaman, if that answers your question.'

'Well, it doesn't. Are you *alive*?'

'I have no idea what you're talking about,' he replied in a singsong voice, but I didn't have the patience for coy games. I went straight up to him and put a hand on his cheek.

Sa-wol looked me in the eye, like he hadn't expected that. 'What are you doing?'

There was one easy way to figure out if he was alive or dead.

'Yeon-hwa, what—'

SLAP!

The impact was almost refreshing. Then came a heavy silence, and Sa-wol grabbed my wrist with a grimace. 'What was that for?'

His cheek was turning red, which meant he had to be among the living. I'd taken the first customer a bit too literally about the Hwawoldang being a place to send off the dead. I bowed my head. 'I'm sorry, Sa-wol. I can't necessarily tell the dead apart from the living.'

Sa-wol put one hand on his aching cheek and leaned in so close that our noses almost touched. I braced myself.

But he grinned, as though *he'd* slapped me and not the other way around. I wanted to step back, but was stopped by the wall. By the time I realized just how long his eyelashes were, my cheeks were just as flushed as his.

'I make sure to pay back my debts,' Sa-wol said. 'I'd have given you a slap for a slap if I hadn't made that promise to your grandmother.'

'What promise?'

'She wanted me to help you,' he replied, and let his smile fade as he stood up straight. That was when I noticed the string of prayer beads around his slender wrist.

'With what, exactly?'

'That,' Sa-wol said, his hand protectively cradling his cheek, 'is between your late grandmother, me, and my brother, who's studying overseas.'

But I couldn't pretend that was enough information. With one finger on my lip, I asked, 'So is this place, like, cursed? I heard even the estate agents don't want to touch it.'

Sa-wol replied, 'Not at all. Actually, this shop is filled with your grandmother's spiritual powers.'

'*Spiritual powers?* My grandmother?'

'She just never told you, I suppose,' Sa-wol said.

'But she probably went through a possession ritual when she was young, or had some innate energy in her bloodline. But instead of becoming a shaman like most people with those abilities, she decided to run this shop – and gave me some of her powers, too.'

My hair stood on end. No one had told me that Grandma was born with a shaman's destiny. She'd never acted strange, never even pasted the usual talismans around the house. The Grandma I remembered was so ordinary that she could blend into any crowd on any street.

'But don't worry,' Sa-wol went on, 'you don't seem to have those powers yourself.'

That was a comfort, but I had more pressing things on my mind. 'More importantly,' I said, 'do you know about her debt? Her will said that she had a way for me to pay it off. What is it, and where can I find it? I can't sit around waiting for the interest to build up.'

'Patience, Yeon-hwa,' Sa-wol said sagely. 'Your grandmother wanted things done in order, and I want things done the way your grandmother wanted.'

'What *are* you to her?'

Sa-wol ran his fingers over his prayer beads, and for an instant the beads seemed to sparkle like amber in his hand.

'She saved my life. And so did you.'

'What?' I didn't understand. He looked so wistful.

'There's no need to be impatient. You'll find out in time.'

Then he smiled again, as if he didn't care how desperate I was, as if he knew exactly what I was thinking. But I could tell that this was very personal for him. So I let it drop.

Though I couldn't help but wonder: when did I ever save someone's life? The most virtuous thing I'd ever done was make a UNICEF donation with my scholarship back in university. But that was only 100,000 won . . . that couldn't be right.

All I knew for sure was that I'd never met Sa-wol in my life. Had he got me confused with someone else who'd inherited a traditional sweetshop who happened to have the same name as me? Sa-wol sat on a stool on the other side of the counter with his legs crossed and his elbow on his knee, jaw resting on the hand with the prayer beads. Now his face was close to mine again, and my gaze followed his smooth complexion and jawline to the collar of his hanbok.

I glimpsed a red scar. It looked like an old abrasion.

Sa-wol must have noticed, because he quickly

tightened his jacket and pointedly changed the subject. 'So what did last night's customer order?'

'Chocolate-covered jeonbyeong.'

'And how did she look in the end?'

'She was smiling,' I said. 'Like she was at peace.'

'You did well, Yeon-hwa. She couldn't have passed on that way without your help.'

I didn't understand. 'But she died horribly and left her poor daughter behind. All I did was make her some jeonbyeong and dip them in chocolate.'

'Every death is a tragedy,' Sa-wol replied in a playful tone. 'But not every spirit can pass on with a smile. You gave her that final piece of satisfaction.'

There was something sweet and silky about his voice, like a sip of hot cocoa. He really meant what he said. Behind the playfulness, I could sense his encouragement. I didn't know if I deserved that comfort.

Taking a deep breath, Sa-wol rose to his feet. But was I up for this?

'Sa-wol, wait!' I said. 'I can't do this alone.'

He frowned, and pointed at the door. 'Didn't think you'd get another one so soon,' he said.

The chime rang, and a new customer entered.

The customer was a man about Sa-wol's age, but much taller. And unlike the pale Sa-wol, he had a healthy, tanned complexion. The customer had straight, dark-brown hair with eyes to match, and eyebrows as thick as his fingers. He reminded me of a chestnut roasted to perfection.

'Um . . . is this the Hwawoldang?' the man asked, awkwardly scratching the back of his neck as he looked around. He'd obviously never set foot in a traditional sweetshop in life.

Sa-wol placed a gentle hand on my shoulder. 'Ms Manager. You're staring a little too hard into his face.'

'H-he's a customer, I'm supposed to pay attention to him,' I hissed.

'Not like *that*, you're not.'

How was I supposed to help myself? I shot Sa-wol a glare and resolved to remember this for when *he* decided to take a second staring at an attractive customer. There was nothing wrong with being dazzled by a good-looking stranger, even if he was probably a ghost.

A ghost. I regained my senses and slapped my cheeks, remembering that maybe I shouldn't be so distracted by the dead, even if they happened to be impossibly handsome. 'Y-yes!' I replied. 'This is the Hwawoldang. How can I help you?'

'I . . . um . . . I don't want to scare you, but . . . well . . . I'm . . . um . . . a ghost, and . . .'

'Yes, we know.'

The man sighed in relief. 'Oh, thank goodness! I'd feel terrible if you fainted or something.'

I didn't expect such a confident-looking man to sound so nervous. But the awkward smile on his face was endearing. The truth was, I was still a little scared, but I put on a brave face to put him at ease – which was only possible thanks to Sa-wol the shaman standing in front of me. If I'd been alone, I might have had a heart attack.

As if on cue, the customer turned to Sa-wol. 'A-are you dead too, sir?' he asked, prodding at the golden bell hanging from his belt.

Sa-wol crossed his arms and gave him an irritated look. 'I'm a *shaman*, thank you. And why the *sir*? You're clearly older than me.'

'S-sorry!' the customer stammered. 'I thought – I thought you might be twenty-nine or so.'

'Ghastly,' Sa-wol replied impishly. 'How old are you?'

'Twenty-six.'

Sa-wol frowned. 'Damn, so I *am* older than you. But I don't look it. Don't you think, Ms Manager?' he asked, turning and pointing from himself to the customer and back. But the customer clearly looked twenty-six, and younger than Sa-wol.

'I don't mind looking older than my age,' the customer said sheepishly.

Sa-wol was completely silenced. His nostrils flared.

This man was almost as young as me when he died. Twenty-six was much too early. The age when people didn't mind looking older than they were – even enjoyed it sometimes. Sa-wol seemed to think the same, because he didn't say another teasing word.

'I . . . um . . . wanted to order a gift box.'

'Of course!' I replied. 'What would you like inside?'

'I don't know much about traditional sweets,' the customer said. 'Something . . . sweet, I guess. And . . .'

'And . . . ?'

'. . . and pretty to look at . . . ?'

'Sweet and pretty to look at,' I repeated. 'Is this for a girlfriend?'

The customer waved his hands, clearly embarrassed. 'N-no, it's not like that,' he said unconvincingly. 'She . . . she wasn't my girlfriend. I . . .'

'. . . never got to ask her out!' Sa-wol finished, slapping him on the back.

'I . . . I think I did, actually, but . . .'

'Wait, what does that mean?' I asked.

'. . . Well . . . I . . . um . . .'

'Please, just tell us!'

The customer hesitated, like he was ashamed to talk about himself. When he finally opened his mouth to speak, he closed it again, then opened and closed it once more.

Sa-wol lost his patience first. 'Out with it, *young man*! And if you can't tell us, we'll have to take a peek ourselves,' he said, and placed his bell on the counter.

'With this thing?'

'Put your finger on the bell,' Sa-wol instructed, gesturing. 'You too, Yeon-hwa.'

Sa-wol and the customer were ready, fingers extended. I remembered that I'd held hands with the customer the other night when I looked into her past, and realized we needed to be in physical contact, or connected somehow through something special like Sa-wol's bell.

I pressed my index finger against the metal surface. 'All right, I'll help you choose the perfect sweet once we've heard your story,' I said reassuringly.

The customer nodded, and told us his name.

The scent of a certain flower filled the shop, and my mind was pulled into the past.

❁

Mae-hyeon never liked his name.

Born into the Jang family, his name was made up of the Chinese characters for 'plum blossom' and 'radiant'. His maternal grandmother had given him the name because the white plum blossoms blooming in the yard on the day he was born had been so bright they could light up the dark. That wasn't much comfort. Other boys had names like Dae-hyeon or Myeong-hyeon, or Tae-hyeon or Woo-hyeon. Why the *flower*? His complexion was the wrong colour for the name, too, because he was ruddy from spending every hour of his childhood out on the basketball courts.

If he never became a professional basketball player, he thought, it would be because of his name.

Mae-hyeon had always been tall for his age, and soon the basketball was his best friend. Even in high school, he'd been a promising talent on the court. He was usually one of the MVP candidates at inter-high tournaments. One hundred and eighty-nine centimetres tall, he played forward – a critical role where he led offensive plays and secured points for the team. But as time went on, he began to feel like he wasn't the right fit for such an aggressive position.

I can feel people watching my every move. And it scares me.

Mae-hyeon was too shy for his own good.

He'd been an ordinary, talkative child. But with each year that passed, he became more and more self-conscious. He'd thought he was an energetic puppy, but learned that he was actually a skittish cat. Soon he couldn't stand performing before the crowds. He couldn't take a shot without pausing.

This is embarrassing. I bet no one else on the court worries about this stuff.

It was such a minor problem, he thought. Nothing worth talking to his teachers about. He didn't want to waste anyone's time with something he knew would disappear soon. But things never did get better, and his teammates only made things worse.

'I don't get it, Mae-hyeon. You're a beast in practice, so why do you mess up in tournaments?'

'You could've got that three-pointer, easy.'

'Look, if you want to keep retreating to the centre, at least help us with the defence.'

Mae-hyeon was objectively talented. He also had an unusually long reach and could jump further than most. Players and coaches alike agreed that he had the perfect build for the sport – which only made the pressure worse. People could forgive poor performance from lousy players, but not from someone who was obviously born to play basketball.

He managed to grit his teeth through high school, though, surrounded by the teammates and instructors who'd been with him throughout those years. He'd also got good enough grades to make it into a sports programme at a university known across the country for its basketball team. He still loved basketball. It was his favourite sport and his greatest skill.

But the anxiety only got worse. By university, he was starting to shy away from his own teammates. He just couldn't seem to make friends with them. It took him time to get to know them, and even longer to learn to work with them.

Naturally, his performance suffered. Rookie mistakes at shooting and passing were par for the course, and his defence was full of holes – and not because the opposing teams were particularly good. As more time passed, Mae-hyeon began to fear competing against other young men his age who bounded forward and shouted loudly in his direction.

Unfortunately, Mae-hyeon was just one of those people – the born singers who couldn't squeak out a note on stage, the dancers who grooved only in their showers, and the writers whose minds went blank when they finally got a book deal. People everywhere were born with the fear of displaying their own talents. He happened to be one of those people, afraid of doing what he knew best.

'Mae-hyeon, you're not cut out for this.'

'I'm sorry, Coach. I promise I'll train harder.'

'It's not a matter of practice. You just don't have what it takes.'

'But, Coach, basketball is all I know.'

'. . . Listen, Mae-hyeon. You know what you look like out there on the court? A *tree*. You look great standing there, but there's not much you can do except wave your stiff branches. . . . No offence about your name, I mean.'

In the end, Mae-hyeon was forced to give up. And one niggling thought remained where his hopes had been: that if he'd been named anything else – Dae-hyeon, Tae-hyeon, or even Woo-hyeon – things might have been different.

In his mid-twenties, Mae-hyeon hated looking back on the past. He wished he'd buckled down to study instead of taking basketball so seriously. He should never have made basketball his dream. Now all he had was the remaining half of his twenties and a blank résumé. A sports graduate who couldn't find a decent job didn't have many options.

'C'mon, Mae-hyeon. There's plenty of things to do. Like getting a social life, for one. You've never dated a girl in your life.'

'I did, in the second year of junior high.'

'That was *ages* ago, man.'

'But it still counts.'

'Not if you didn't kiss her.'

'We were *fifteen*!'

'Didn't even hold hands?'

'. . . No.'

'You know what people call that? "Playing house".'

'Asshole.'

Mae-hyeon had spent all his time either on the basketball court or at home. He remembered nothing else. His first ever crush was probably on his teacher, but he didn't even remember which. His first *love* was basketball, and he'd fallen in love at first sight with his brand-new basketball jersey.

By the time the hair he'd cropped for basketball had grown out to cover his ears, Mae-hyeon wanted to take back his youth. It wasn't too late, he thought. He should try everything he'd missed out on – work, dreams, love, friendship, anything. He wrote cover letters, studied for his English qualifications, got all the basic licences, and spent his spare time taking long showers and putting on cologne. He was busy every day applying for jobs, but went out to every blind date his friends set him up on. He mostly liked the girls he met.

Mae-hyeon tried to picture a new future: going to work in a slick suit at a big-name company, and holding hands with a woman he loved.

But even now, he couldn't stop feeling anxious.

We regret to inform you that your application has not been selected . . .

I'm sorry, but I prefer men who take the lead . . .

Reality loved to let people down, and Mae-hyeon was no exception. He had many applications rejected, many dates declined, and many dreams crushed.

'You're such a wallflower, man. Be more assertive.'

'How?'

'Just . . . keep throwing yourself into those situations. It'll work out.'

'. . . Really?'

'Come on, stand up straight! You're putting your shoulders to waste.'

His friends assured him that he just needed to work up a bit of courage. That a former athlete like him had every reason to be confident. Mae-hyeon agreed. The person who stared back in his mirror was a *man*, not a boy, and a tall and well-built one. What did he have to be afraid of?

But the fear never went away.

He was still afraid of talking to strangers, and broke into a cold sweat when people looked in his direction. He didn't understand. He was so ready to do his best and experience as much as he could, but his body wouldn't listen. Like an unemotional person pretending to be sentimental, or an extrovert pretending to be an introvert, Mae-hyeon could not help his nature.

When his courage failed him, he tried again, only to have it fail him again.

We apologize . . .

I'm sorry . . .

Soon his opportunities were dwindling.

He resigned himself to his fate. His dreams of basketball were long gone, and he barely made any effort with his job applications. He deleted his instant messaging accounts and wiped most of his contacts list. Like a bear in hibernation, he curled up in his blankets.

Life turned into monochrome as he stayed warm at home in spring, chilly at home under the AC in summer, cool at home in autumn, and toasty by the heater in winter. Even his mother lost patience at that point, slapping him on the back and shouting at him to do *something* useful with his life.

He was twenty-six years old, and another meaningless spring had come upon the world.

'Mae-hyeon, I've got a favour to ask,' said Gyu-tae, one of his best friends. Mae-hyeon had cut most people out of his life, but Gyu-tae lived in the same neighbourhood and would not give up on him. 'My hiking club's meeting up next week, but my uncle got sick and I have to go visit him. Can you fill in for me this time?'

'It's just a hike. What do you need a sub for?'

'C'mon, man. They hired a bus, but they need to fill up the seats or the bus company's going to cancel. Someone's gotta be there.'

'. . . I don't feel like it.'

'What if I gave you 50,000 won? Better than your mum calling you a deadbeat. What do you say?'

❀

When Mae-hyeon woke up on the morning of the hike, he was filled with regrets. *Shit, why did I agree to this? I'm not going to know anyone there, and they're not going to talk to me.* But the thought of getting chewed out by his mother reminded him that he couldn't back out now. He had to show her he was being productive, even if it was with a single 50,000-won bill.

The weather was so beautiful that it seemed to taunt him. Cherry blossoms were in full bloom all around, turning the world into a sea of blue and pink as Mae-hyeon stood awkwardly at the parking lot. In the distance, he spotted fifteen or so people who could only be from the hiking club. They were all laughing and chattering.

'Excuse me . . .'

'Can I help you?'

'I . . . um . . . I'm Gyu-tae's . . .'

'You're Gyu-tae?'

'N-no, I'm his friend. My name's Jang Mae-hyeon.'

'Ah! I see your name on the roster. Welcome to the club! It's nice to meet you.'

'Th-thank you.'

'Wow, you're so tall!'

The woman who greeted Mae-hyeon had light brown hair cut into a bob. She gestured at his height, but when Mae-hyeon stepped back awkwardly, she withdrew her hand. Then the others crowded around, saying hello to Mae-hyeon and introducing themselves one after another. They all looked as pleasant as the weather.

'Great to have you with us today,' said a man who seemed to be about Mae-hyeon's age, offering a handshake. 'Did you remember to read the rules?'

It struck Mae-hyeon how outgoing everyone seemed to be. The whole club talked loudly and excitedly, and he felt so out of place that he wanted to go home. 'I . . . no, I didn't know . . .'

The man smiled, and introducing himself as the chairman of the club, explained, 'That's all right! All you need to know is that we always hike in pairs to make sure no one gets left behind.' Then he pointed to the woman who'd been looking at the roster. 'Today, you're with Seo-hui, our admin!'

According to the chairman, Seo-hui was twenty

years old, and in charge of administrative tasks at the hiking club. Mae-hyeon didn't feel up to making conversation with the woman he'd backed away from, but not because he didn't like her. He was just ashamed and embarrassed.

It wasn't long before the club members piled into the bus, and Seo-hui gestured Mae-hyeon inside. She had to sit in the front because she was in charge of the supplies, and as her partner for the day, Mae-hyeon sat at the front as well. He didn't know what he'd got himself into. He didn't know anything about the club or its members, and he didn't enjoy hiking. Not to mention the fact that he didn't know what mountain they were headed to. He wished he hadn't sold his day for 50,000 won and wondered if it was too late to throw himself out the window.

'So where are you coming from?'

'M-me? I . . . just from home.'

'Where do you live?'

'The Sinsu-dong neighbourhood.'

'Oh, hey! I know that area. There's a really affordable galbitang restaurant there, have you been?'

'Gwangheungchang Galbitang?'

'Yeah, but I always have the seolleongtang stew

instead of the marinated ribs. The broth is so flavourful, but it's not too salty . . .'

Seo-hui could talk forever. She asked question after question and answered questions he never asked, until Mae-hyeon felt like his exhausted soul was floating away from his body. But still, he was happy that she went on talking. He couldn't stand awkward silences.

'Um . . . so about Gyu-tae. You sound like you don't know him.'

'Who's Gyu-tae?'

Mae-hyeon's jaw dropped. 'I – I thought he was in this club. He said the bus would get cancelled if not enough people showed up.'

'What? We chartered the whole bus, not individual seats. They'd take us even if only one person showed up today. And no, I don't know any Gyu-tae. Your name was on the list of new applicants, though.'

The smile on her face was so bright and innocent that Mae-hyeon felt like an idiot – which he was. He finally realized that his situation had been planned to perfection by his mischievous best friend.

The hiking club was far from hardcore. Everyone went at their own pace, and soon the members had split into smaller groups of similar speeds. The group in the lead was full of energy, and singing a song to match the weather as their feet pumped up and down the trail. The groups near the middle chattered endlessly even as they went up the slope. Even the steepest mountains couldn't put a dent in the friends' conversations.

Seo-hui and Mae-hyeon found themselves at the very back.

This isn't that hard, Mae-hyeon thought. With his years of training, he could sprint all the way to the peak without blinking, the mountain breeze rushing through his hair. But he didn't want to stand out. So he slouched as much as he could and went up the trail at a crawl, pretending that his muscles meant nothing when it came to hiking. No one suspected a thing.

Seo-hui, though, didn't have to fool anyone.

'Ugh, this is killing me!'

She was climbing her heart out, but just couldn't keep up with the group, no matter how many chocolate breaks, breath-catching breaks and leg-massage breaks she took. And because he'd been assigned as her partner, Mae-hyeon had to take breaks with her.

'You can go on ahead without me, Mae-hyeon,' Seo-hui insisted.

'No, it's all right . . .'

'It's *not* all right. I'll be fine, so you should go say hi to the other people, too.'

'. . . I . . . I don't have to do that.'

He was glad to wait for Seo-hui. He hadn't wanted to stand out too much by going ahead, and thought hanging back was the best way to avoid attention.

Damn it, Gyu-tae. Why do you have to poke your nose into my life?

Part of him resented his old friend for shoving him into this predicament. But Mae-hyeon soon realized that Gyu-tae wouldn't have gone this far if he hadn't looked so pathetic. All he could do now was keep on hiking. There was no turning back time.

'I should've brought water,' Seo-hui gasped.

'H-here, I brought some.'

'Oh, thanks,' she replied. 'Samdasoo water? I love this brand! I swear, it's my favourite . . .'

Seo-hui went on talking again, sometimes to herself and sometimes trying to start a conversation. And she constantly stopped and asked him to take pictures.

'One more, just under that tree!'

'Right.'
'What do you think? Pretty, right?'
'Wh-what?'
'The *flowers*.'
'Oh, um . . . yeah.'

The spring breeze caressed the blossoms hanging from the branches, rattling them like temple bells. Blades of grass brushed together until they created music in the air. The rest of the hiking club had long since gone ahead, but Mae-hyeon and Seo-hui alone took breaks as they climbed, again and again and again.

Mae-hyeon had never seen anyone ask for so many pictures of themselves. And each time he picked up the camera, she even struck a new pose between each click of the shutter. He couldn't believe they were the same *species*. What made her so different? So outgoing, even with a complete stranger? He didn't think he'd ever understand.

Soon it was two in the afternoon. On a normal day, he would usually be lying in bed half-listening to the TV. Three o'clock was when he usually agonized over his uncertain future, four o'clock when he fell into negativity, and five o'clock when he sank into self-loathing. But not today.

A pine-scented gust of wind filled his nostrils. He exhaled and then breathed deeply for the first time in a year.

'You're so good at taking pictures!' Seo-hui exclaimed as she looked over the photos.

'I . . . um . . . I'm glad to hear that.'

'You really have an eye for details; I'm impressed.'

'*Me?*'

Seo-hui pointed at one of the pictures he'd taken. She was right in the middle, and the colours were carefully balanced to highlight the lush hues of the flowers. Mae-hyeon remembered taking all those details into account as he adjusted the settings. 'Yeah,' she replied with a smile. 'I hear shy people are really good at intricate stuff. Now stick close to me, okay? I'll make sure you fit right in with the club.'

Mae-hyeon had to look far down to see Seo-hui's face. He didn't think she could help him fit right in with the rest of the club, not when they were probably hours ahead on the trail. But she shrugged and looked up with unfounded confidence. He chuckled, but how could he not be grateful? Unlike him, she'd seen something good in his character. He just hadn't expected that from someone so much smaller than himself, who could barely hike a mountain trail.

She was adorable.

They continued up the mountain, finally reaching the midpoint of the trail – and the public bathrooms, outside which Mae-hyeon spotted a garbage can. Finally getting the chance to toss their trash, he placed it all into a plastic bag, tied up the opening, and – letting his guard down – tossed it into the can as if shooting a basketball.

The little bag of trash flew in an elegant arc and landed in the garbage can without even touching the rim. Seo-hui burst into applause.

'Wow, Mae-hyeon! You looked just like a basketball player!'

That's because I was *a basketball player*, Mae-hyeon wanted to brag, but all he could do was smile awkwardly.

Seo-hui knew the names of all the trees by heart. *That's an oak tree. That one's a pine tree, and that one over there's a willow*. But when the path took them up a slope, most of her explanations were drowned out by tired gasps – until she finally tripped on a rock and slipped. She seemed to have twisted something badly, and Mae-hyeon laughed in disbelief as he picked this stranger up off the ground and carried her on his back.

'Hey, you look so much better when you smile,' Seo-hui said, not realizing just how embarrassed he was. 'I bet you were really popular in school.'

'M-me? No, not at all.'

'No, I bet all the girls liked you, even if you didn't know it. Trust me, we notice faces like yours.'

Seo-hui was one surprise after another. Mae-hyeon's friends had told him he was good-looking, but he'd always thought they were just being nice.

Mae-hyeon surprised Seo-hui too. She knew she shouldn't judge a book by its cover, but she'd never met anyone so different from his looks. She liked that about him. She was not the type to hide her feelings. She expressed her opinions openly. For her, feelings were not meant to be considered and reconsidered for weeks or months at a time.

A plum tree stood ahead, some of its flowers still in bloom. Mae-hyeon let Seo-hui down for a rest, and she limped to the shade of the tree. As she fanned her heated face, she gestured for him to join her.

Mae-hyeon, though, stood where he was and took in the scene. Was it because of Seo-hui? For once in his life, he was impressed by a plum tree.

'I have a question,' Seo-hui said, as he came near.
'Wh-what is it?'
'Do you have a girlfriend?'

Mae-hyeon's gaze trembled, violently. Seo-hui burst into laughter, like she was watching a waddling toddler, and Mae-hyeon froze as quickly as the last time he'd let an opponent score a three-point shoot.

But he wouldn't mind if she went on shooting more.

❦

Seo-hui was sunshine.

The second she'd got his number, she asked him about his weekend plans and proposed getting lunch together and taking a stroll through the park.

What a weird girl.

Before he knew it, he'd had her number memorized, waited for the weekend, had lunch with her, and was strolling through the park with her. He would have been happy to spend time like that with anyone, but the fact that it was *Seo-hui* made it even better. He couldn't believe Seo-hui and her eternally sunny smile could enjoy the company of a man like him.

They went on meeting regularly through the spring.

'So what kind of girl is your type, Mae-hyeon? You never tell me these things.'

Seo-hui never ran out of questions, which meant she wanted to learn more about him. The only difference was that now she could text him with those questions too.

'A girl with a nice personality, I guess.'

'Guys who say that always have crazy high standards.'

'So does liking you mean a guy has high standards?'

'Hm?'

'N-no, what I meant was . . . um . . . I . . .'

'Are you zoning out again, Mae-hyeon?'

Mae-hyeon panicked. They'd gone out to eat and watch movies together multiple times, but they weren't officially dating. He'd never told anyone outside his family that he loved them, and couldn't believe he'd almost crossed that line. And he knew: hiding his feelings would only get harder.

'Wh-what about you?' he asked, not because he wanted to change the subject, but because now he was curious about her too.

'Oh, you want to know *my* type?' Seo-hui replied with a sly grin. 'A responsible man! I just live with my mum now because my father gave us such a hard time. I want someone who actually takes care of his family and pulls more than his weight.'

The bright smile on her face didn't mean her life was all roses. Mae-hyeon's heart ached even more to know that the pain in Seo-hui's life was so completely hidden by her relentlessly upbeat attitude. *Maybe that's why I feel this way.* He thought back to the sight of Seo-hui on the mountain, sitting next to the plum tree. She was even more real now, even more human, and he wanted to help her.

'Obviously, that doesn't mean I'm going to be irresponsible,' Seo-hui went on. 'I want to be responsible in everything I do, too. D-does that make me sound too serious?'

'Not at all.'

Seo-hui looked down. 'Thanks, but sometimes I think it makes me unattractive. That's what the guy at my last blind date said. He said I was too uptight, like I should be more playful.'

Without a word, Mae-hyeon put a gentle hand on her head, as though comforting a nervous puppy. Even when she doubted herself, she was nothing less than lovely. Seo-hui looked up in happy surprise.

He didn't think he was the most responsible

person. But now he wanted to be. He knew that he could try to be like Seo-hui and finally make something of his life.

'Seo-hui.'

'Yeah?'

'Remember that picture of you I took on the hiking trip? Would you mind if I made that my phone wallpaper?'

Mae-hyeon was twenty-six years old. And he resolved to make sure twenty-year-old Seo-hui finally got to enjoy a real summer.

❀

One weekday evening, Mae-hyeon called Gyu-tae to meet him at a street stand.

Gyu-tae entered the streetside tent nervously, bracing himself for Mae-hyeon's irritation at signing him up for the hiking club. He'd only wanted to get his friend out of the house, but he was ready to get on his knees and beg for forgiveness if it turned out to have been a bust.

Mae-hyeon sat alone at a round plastic table in the deserted tent. In front of him were two bottles of beer, a plate of dried cuttlefish and a bowl of salted peanuts. He chewed inscrutably on a cuttlefish tentacle, pulling over a white plastic chair when he sensed Gyu-tae's presence.

'Gyu-tae. Sit down.'

Stiffly, Gyu-tae said hello and took his seat. Drinks at a street stand could only mean one thing: the truth was coming out. He gulped.

But Mae-hyeon's question shattered his every expectation.

'Gyu-tae, you had a girlfriend when we were twenty, right? And she was also twenty?'

'Yeah.'

'Did you get each other Valentine's and White Day gifts?'

'Yeah. What's this all about?' Gyu-tae asked, relaxing enough to take a smooth, refreshing sip of beer.

'What about Coming-of-Age Day? Did you give presents for that?'

'. . . You gotta be joking,' Gyu-tae said. He couldn't stop grinning, like a father whose toddler had just told him about a crush on a daycare friend.

Mae-hyeon waved in denial, but he couldn't hide the smile on his face. 'Thanks, man,' he said. 'Thanks for the intervention.'

'Well, shit! Looks like things are finally looking up for you! It's all smooth sailing from here on out.'

'Let's not get too ahead of ourselves.'

Gyu-tae, though, couldn't wipe the grin from his lips. He'd seen Mae-hyeon slowly retreat from the world after retiring from basketball. He was happy to help. Signing him up for a hiking club without asking might have been going too far, but at the end of the day, it had worked out. Mae-hyeon was one step further from another day wasted in bed with his phone.

'All right,' Gyu-tae said firmly. 'Drinks are on me today. I'm feeling good, you hear?'

'Thanks, man.'

'I hope this works out for you, I really do.'

'Now tell me what you did for Coming-of-Age Day.'

Gyu-tae said thoughtfully, 'Let's see . . . I gave her flowers and a bottle of perfume. She got me a new wallet.'

'And it felt meaningful, right?' Mae-hyeon asked, urging.

'Of course it did. It was a new start! I mean, we broke up afterwards, but I'm never going to forget the girl I dated when I turned twenty. I still have the wallet at home,' Gyu-tae said, and pulled up his chair closer to the table. 'But last I checked, you were twenty-*six*.'

'. . . *She's* twenty.'

'Cradle robber!' Gyu-tae said jokingly, throwing a peanut into Mae-hyeon's face.

Mae-hyeon dodged it with the reflexes he'd honed for over a decade and replied in a defeated voice, 'It's a little much, huh?'

'I'm kidding.'

'That's a relief.'

'But you'd better be responsible, you hear? You're six years older than her. You gotta pull your weight.'

'Responsible, huh?'

'That's the most important thing in a relationship,' Gyu-tae declared. 'Not money, *responsibility*.'

Mae-hyeon downed the rest of his beer and turned the word over in his mind. If both Seo-hui *and* Gyu-tae thought responsibility was so important, he knew that was what he had to pursue.

'So,' Gyu-tae said, 'what does she like, anyway?'

'. . . Not hiking. We haven't gone since the day we met.'

'Good to know what she *doesn't* like, but let's try to think of something she'll appreciate.'

Mae-hyeon fell into thought once more. What did Seo-hui like? She seemed to like both tomato sauce and alfredo sauce when they went for pasta, and she enjoyed lamb and pork just the same. She liked everything people her age liked. But did that mean she didn't have any favourites at all? He realized that he didn't really know what she *loved*. Seo-hui only ever smiled in front of him. She'd never looked unhappy as she chattered next to him, walked with him, and met his gaze.

The truth hit him like a ton of bricks.

'I think . . .' he said hesitantly, '. . . I think she likes me.'

'Speak up, I can't hear you.'

'I think she likes *me*.'

'Asshole!' Gyu-tae teased again, pelting him with one peanut after another, a jealous grin on his face. Mae-hyeon dodged them all. Gyu-tae calmed down and added, 'Be good to her, you hear?'

'Of course I—'

'Even *more* than you think you need to be. She's only twenty.'

'I *know* that. There's a lot of responsibility being the older—'

'That's not what I'm talking about. Twenty's a

special age, you know? And this twenty-year-old likes *you*. Be responsible and decent. Take this seriously, and don't get lazy just because you don't have to win her over anymore. It's really sweet, you know? When someone likes you enough that you can feel it without them telling you.'

Gyu-tae was lecturing him, but Mae-hyeon didn't mind. He nodded meekly, knowing that he wanted to do right by Seo-hui – not because she was younger, or because she was a woman, but because he wanted to repay her for accepting him as he was.

❀

Flowers and perfume, Gyu-tae had insisted, and Mae-hyeon flushed deep red as he thought about his plan. He felt like he might get struck by lightning if he asked Seo-hui out, as though doing something different for once was going to destroy him. He almost laughed and shook with fear when he thought of saying something that cheesy to her.

But the thought made him happy anyway.

'Here comes the next batch.'

Now money was his only problem.

'Right, sir!'

'Chop chop! This is the busy season; every second counts.'

Because he had no savings, he decided to do day work at a logistics centre. All he had to do was sort packages for shipping. It required no thought and paid quickly. Mae-hyeon had never made 100,000 won a day before, and because he was scared his family and friends might tell him to find a more comfortable job, he didn't tell anyone where he was working.

'Always think of the next person in the line,' the manager said, tapping Mae-hyeon on the back. 'Don't pause for a second; one hold-up can clog the entire operation.'

The tsunami of packages on the line left Mae-hyeon scrambling. No one said a word as they sorted their goods, like they'd all been turned into cogs in a gigantic machine. He spent the entire shift bent forward, picking up and tossing and picking up and tossing box after box. His arms were numb, and sweat flooded down his face.

But he couldn't stop his stupid grin. His arms were about to burst, but he didn't care; it was nothing compared to carrying Seo-hui up the mountain. He couldn't believe such hard work made him so happy.

Mae-hyeon vowed that he would always feed Seo-hui until she couldn't eat any more.

Three night shifts later, he had 300,000 won in hand – more than enough to buy flowers and perfume, on top of a nice day out. On his final day at the logistics centre, he stepped out of the building during his break to contact Seo-hui.

Want to meet up on Saturday? I'll see you at the park.

A bead of sweat fell from his chin as he lied, writing to say he was up so late because he couldn't sleep. He reached up to wipe the rest of the sweat, but fumbled and dropped his phone.

It plopped right down into the storm drain.

Of all the places!

The little device, his only connection with Seo-hui, disappeared into the dark. Mae-hyeon tried to lift the cover, but realized that he needed to raise it with a lever. But the sound of rushing water below made him anxious. What if the phone got carried away? He would never find it again. And he had no intention of spending his hard-earned money on a new phone.

My arm might just be long enough, he thought, and took a deep breath.

The drain was much shallower than he'd thought.

He felt sloshing water at his fingertips, and knew that he could fish up his phone if he just reached a little further.

Come on . . . come on . . .

Mae-hyeon pressed himself even flatter against the pavement, his face glued to the drain to see better.

Then there was light, and he could see into the drain. Someone seemed to be casting a torch in his direction – and he saw his phone. Mae-hyeon smiled. It was so close, just within reach –

'Hey, you there!'

He looked up. He didn't see a person with a torch.

The headlights of a delivery truck barrelled towards him.

❦

We pulled away from the bell at the same time.

It was hard to find the right words. I couldn't even offer comfort, because that might sound like I was only trying to make myself feel better.

But Sa-wol didn't seem to have any awareness.

'Poor old Mae-hyeon,' he said dramatically. 'You died before you went on a proper date!'

I was surprised to see Mae-hyeon nod. He pulled

out his phone, and with a deep breath, showed us the wallpaper. A woman smiled under a blossoming tree on one brilliant spring day.

Mae-hyeon explained that no one had found his phone after he died. And since he'd been too shy to introduce Seo-hui to anyone in his life, she hadn't found out until much later that he was gone.

I couldn't believe my ears. 'But that's ridiculous. How does that happen in this day and age?'

'That's how the world of the living works sometimes,' Mae-hyeon replied bitterly, scratching his head. 'I was pretty ridiculous too. What kind of athlete is chronically shy?'

My heart ached. It was like Mae-hyeon was beating himself up, when he'd already been through so much. He didn't let it show, though. It seemed like death had brought him peace. He added, 'That's how life is. Just one ridiculous thing after another.'

He went on to explain how painful it had been, thinking of how Seo-hui must have waited for him for hours on that fateful Saturday. Today was the third anniversary of his death. The dead were supposed to come to the Hwawoldang within forty-nine days of dying, but he'd lingered by Seo-hui all this time out of guilt.

'Now I see,' I said. 'That's why you placed that order.'

'Yeah. I want something just as sweet and beautiful as she is.'

I took a determined breath. 'And we'll make that happen!'

I knew exactly what to make. Inside Grandma's recipe booklet, I found instructions for flower-shaped manju buns – sweet little desserts shaped like flowers or fruits. They were lovely to look at – the perfect gift for a loved one. The booklet had recipes for camellia, cherry blossom and sunflower, but I wanted something different.

'Plum blossoms,' I declared, and got to work.

I kneaded white bean paste into dough, then combined it with glutinous rice powder and water before microwaving the mixture for shaping. For other flowers, I would have to add food colouring for the petals; but the bean paste was already as white as the plum blossoms I wanted. All I had to do was add a bit of yellow to the centre of each flower for the stamen. Plum blossoms looked similar to cherry blossoms, but their petals were curved instead of forked at the ends. I thought of Mae-hyeon's wallpaper and tried to make them as round as the smile on the woman's face.

With manju buns, appearances mattered more than deep textures and flavours. It wasn't long before I had five lovely blossoms sitting in compartments of a small cypress box, all wrapped up and ready to hand over.

'How do you like them?' I asked proudly, holding out one extra manju I'd prepared for tasting.

Mae-hyeon took a bite out of the sweet extra bun and grinned. 'This is great! I know she'll love it. But how are you going to get this to her?'

'Delivery's not part of the service here,' Sa-wol cut in, irritated. 'Which most of the dead don't seem to realize when they drop in.'

Mae-hyeon deflated. 'I wish she could try a bite of this, too,' he sighed, but didn't seem to want to argue. He reminded me of a sad golden retriever.

'Then let me do it!' I volunteered.

'Whaaaat?' Sa-wol cried dramatically. 'How?'

'With *your* help!'

'Nuh-uh, leave me out of this! When your grandmother passed, I swore I wouldn't let you rope me in like she did!' He complained about Grandma guilting him into 'helping a frail old woman'. Now he refused to lift another finger.

Mae-hyeon looked more and more downcast

with each second that passed. I couldn't take it anymore.

'Sa-wol!' I said sharply. 'Look at the poor man! This is his final request! He's already dead!'

'Yes, he's already dead. Which is why you should consider *not* being so motivated by his looks.'

'I'm motivated by his *story*, Sa-wol,' I argued. 'You'd have to be heartless to turn down those eyes.'

'So it's his looks after all,' Sa-wol replied, but when I grabbed his hands pleadingly, he shoved the bell into his pocket and nodded. He was a lot softer than he let on, which was probably how Grandma got him to help so much. I didn't dislike that about him.

❋

The plan was simple. All we had to do was find Seo-hui and deliver the manju buns. But Sa-wol would only help on one condition: that Seo-hui never found out that the Hwawoldang connected the dead with the living. Too many curious eyes might chip away at the powers that filled the shop; such special hidden gifts would lose their power if they were revealed.

Mae-hyeon looked disappointed, but Sa-wol

would not budge. 'Listen, young man. We're not running a therapy office for the dead. This delivery job is a special service, do you hear me?'

'Th-then what's the point of all this?' Mae-hyeon stammered. 'I have to let her know how I feel.'

'No,' Sa-wol said flatly. 'Today, we resolve your regrets and finally help you reincarnate. That's what the whole purchase process *is*. By buying sweets from the Hwawoldang, you get yourself a ticket to a new life. Do you understand what that means? Today is your last day as Jang Mae-hyeon, the man who remembers Lee Seo-hui.'

Sa-wol seemed to know all about the workings of the shop, the dead, and the rules they had to follow. I listened, careful not to miss a word.

Meanwhile, the black cat from before appeared outside the shop. She meowed, as if calling to us.

'Would you look at that. The cat knows where Seo-hui is,' said Sa-wol.

I turned. 'She's no normal cat, is she?'

'She's probably got as much spiritual power as I have. Everything comes to this shop for a reason.'

The cat didn't take us far. When we reached the park, Mae-hyeon said that was where he'd met Seo-hui on her days off.

'Very fortunate,' Sa-wol noted. 'She wouldn't have bothered to bring us in person if the park were far. All we could have done was have the manju delivered by dreams.'

'Do you really think this is just a coincidence?'

'What do you mean?'

'Maybe there's, I don't know, some sort of fate connecting the living and the dead,' I speculated.

'Or it's all just a mischievous ghost playing pranks on us.'

We placed the box of flower-shaped manju on a bench lit by a streetlight. We didn't see anyone, but Sa-wol dusted off the surface of the bench anyway. 'She'll be here soon, I suppose.'

'Sir,' Mae-hyeon said suddenly, 'could I borrow your body for a bit?'

'What?'

'The lady here doesn't seem to have any power at all, but you're a shaman. I can see your spirit gate clearly.'

'Uh, I don't much feel like being possessed –'

The black cat gave a sharp cry and popped into the bushes. I followed after her. At the same time, I saw Mae-hyeon's body overlap with Sa-wol, who suddenly complained about a headache.

He'd been possessed. I hissed at him to pick up the cypress box.

'Of all the incorrigible . . .' Sa-wol muttered, clutching his head.

A woman approached from the distance. She was petite, but her arms swung wildly with each step and there was something charming about the way she walked. This had to be Seo-hui – and she was three sheets to the wind.

She half-collapsed onto the bench, and Sa-wol pinched his nose at the stink of alcohol. 'Good gods, at least have the decency to go straight home after your hundredth drink.'

She looked up with hazy eyes. 'What'd you say to me, old guy?'

'*Old guy?*' Sa-wol repeated angrily, but he seemed to have recognized who Seo-hui was, too.

Meanwhile, Seo-hui pushed herself into a seated position and slurred, 'Don't talk to me, okay? I got stood up real bad.'

I was still peering out from the foliage across the way, and gave Sa-wol an encouraging look. He crossed his arms and knitted his brow. 'You're *sitting* on this bench, as far as I can tell.'

'Hey, I'm not taking sass from a total stranger.'

'I wouldn't call myself a total stranger. Some irresponsible young man just told me he stood up the girl he liked.'

' "Irresponsible" doesn't *begin* to describe that shitty flake!'

Sa-wol's shoulders twitched, probably because of Mae-hyeon's influence.

Seo-hui sighed, drooping feebly. 'Why's love gotta be so hard, mister?' she asked, hanging her head. But her cheeks still glowed so red I could see them under the streetlight.

'Now, what makes you say that?'

'It's just – the guy I liked left me years ago. And I never dated anyone after that.'

'What? A decent-looking girl like you?'

'I don't know,' Seo-hui sighed. 'Maybe they can tell I'm still not over what happened.'

A different look came over Sa-wol's eyes. He stepped closer. 'What happened to you?'

'My first love. He died three years ago.'

'Did you resent him for it?'

'I hated his guts.'

He laughed. 'Then I guess he's headed straight to hell.'

'He'd better be!' Seo-hui roared, but she paused.

Then she was slurring again, this time downcast. 'No . . . no, that's not true. He can't go to hell. He was such a sweet guy. You know what? I hope he's gone to heaven. I hope he can forget me and be happy up there.'

Bit by bit, she began to nod off. Her slurring slowed even more.

'Wish I could follow him there. Twenty-three years old and not a single real relationship.'

'You make it sound like you've failed.'

'Because . . . because nobody loves me as much as my first love did. And I can't seem to love anyone as much as I loved him.'

With Sa-wol's hands, Mae-hyeon fidgeted with the cypress manju box. And he stared into Seo-hui's face. She'd almost dozed off completely, partly lost to her dreams.

Even half-asleep, she was beautiful.

'But I want you to find love in this life,' Mae-hyeon said, placing his hand on hers.

Seo-hui said nothing. She was almost asleep.

'I want you to be happy, Seo-hui. As happy as you made me.'

Then her eyes slid shut completely, and she was leaning entirely on Mae-hyeon's shoulder.

Mae-hyeon smiled with Sa-wol's face and ran a gentle hand across her cheek, considerately laying her down on the bench.

Then he left Sa-wol's body.

I tiptoed out of the bushes as Sa-wol warned Mae-hyeon that he'd run out of time.

'I know,' Mae-hyeon said. 'And I know what I want to do.'

'What?'

'I'll get reincarnated as quickly as possible. Twenty-three years can't be too much of an age difference in a relationship, right?'

I asked, 'Do you really mean that?'

'I do!'

I hadn't seen Mae-hyeon so confident all night. Their bonds had come to an end, but I could see satisfaction in his eyes. He'd told Seo-hui everything he'd wanted to say.

Midnight drew closer, second by heartless second. Sa-wol gave Mae-hyeon a slap on the back and urged him to move on. We'd make sure Seo-hui got home all right.

Mae-hyeon knelt one last time, staring into his first love's face.

'Even if we never meet again,' he whispered, 'I want you to be happy.'

Then, he turned. Mae-hyeon looked almost lonely as he walked away alone. But when we called his name to wave goodbye, he flashed us a brilliant smile.

❀

Mae-hyeon was gone. I shook Seo-hui by the shoulders. 'Excuse me,' I said. 'You shouldn't sleep out here.'

She opened her drowsy eyes and asked what she was doing on a park bench. Sa-wol and I put on the performance of a lifetime, saying we'd just found her drunk in the park. She finally rose with a start, realizing what she was doing, and pulled out her phone.

'My parents are going to kill me!' she cried, realizing it was past midnight, and snatched her bag off the ground.

Just before she could sprint for the taxis lined up on the streets, I pointed to the cypress box. 'Wait, don't forget that!'

'It's not mine!'

'You might not remember, but a gentleman gave you that box,' I said.

Before Seo-hui could argue, we left – and then we stole a backwards glance.

Seo-hui gingerly opened up the box. Her eyes widened.

'Plum blossoms?'

There was a cool breeze, and her eyes narrowed. The love she'd lost hadn't quite let go of her yet.

Sa-wol and I turned our backs again, hoping that the farewell gift would usher in a happy new future for Seo-hui. I wondered if fate would ever reunite them, and looked up at the distant, unanswering stars.

And, like the twenty-year-old Seo-hui, I asked Sa-wol:

'Do you have a girlfriend?'

He stared back without a word. But he couldn't hide the flush of his earlobes.

❦

We found Mae-hyeon's payment at the Hwawoldang: a basketball. The dead seemed to pay for their sweets with objects that had been important to them in life. But the shop wasn't some fantasyland oasis. It was a real, physical shop with a real, physical owner (me), and real bills to pay. Which dresses and basketballs couldn't cover.

'Take those items to Hongseoksa Temple. It's the nearest Buddhist temple in the area. They'll recognize your grandmother's name.'

I frowned. 'A Buddhist temple will buy a dress and a basketball?'

'You can't rely on me for everything,' Sa-wol stated. 'We all learn best by doing, not listening.' Then he gave me the directions to the temple.

What else was I supposed to do? I met up with Yi-ryeong for the first time in ages that Saturday. I told her I was nervous because I'd never been to a temple, and she was happy to come with me. So we dressed for a light hike and headed off at noon. The way up was still moist from the drizzle overnight, and the scent of wet grass and trees filled our nostrils as we marched up the cool path.

'Anyway, how's business doing?'

I groaned. 'I can't believe I *miss* the endless job applications and interviews.'

'It's like your grandma's playing drill instructor from beyond the grave,' Yi-ryeong said with a laugh. 'What's that stuff you're carrying?'

'I have to deliver these.'

'To a *temple*?'

Would Yi-ryeong even believe me if I said the dress

and the basketball were payment from the dead? No, probably not, but if she did, that would be annoying too. Yi-ryeong was always the first to suggest solutions, which in my case would be attempts at exorcisms and gut ceremonies at the shop.

If I didn't want her to worry, I would have to tell a white lie.

'They're like a donation,' I explained with a grin. 'I thought the monks might need a few things.'

Yi-ryeong gave me a curious look, but she was quickly distracted by a vegetarian bibimbap restaurant on the road.

The gentle climb went on for twenty minutes. I was glad Hongseoksa Temple wasn't on some sheer mountaintop. 'Yi-ryeong,' I gasped, 'we really need to work out some more.'

'Yeah,' she replied, 'apparently you have to start when you're young, or you're at a greater risk of heart attacks.'

I shuddered. 'Don't scare me like that!'

'No. You know what's *really* scary? My body fat percentage readout on the scale at the gym!'

But even the horrifying discussion that followed couldn't dent the fresh air, and we didn't mind the sweat on our brows as we skipped up the path. We spread our arms wide along the way, filling every inch of our lungs with the smell of the trees, and felt a comforting, warm sensation on our backs.

Then we saw the temple.

'I don't see any visitors.'

'I guess it's not popular.'

Clear sunlight and silence perched together on the temple roof, and the faint aroma of incense wafted towards us. The temple office in the left-hand corner was empty, probably because it was a weekend.

Yi-ryeong pointed at the main sanctum. 'There. I see a monk.'

Beyond the only open sanctuary door, a monk sat serenely on a cushion. He definitely heard us, but went on meditating with eyelids softly shut. He looked perfectly at peace.

'Excuse me,' I said hesitantly, 'I'm Hong Yeon-hwa from the Hwawoldang.'

The monk's eyes slid open. 'Ah. You would be Mrs Lim's granddaughter, I presume?'

'Yes. Did you know her?'

Slowly, the monk turned to face us. 'I see you've brought the objects,' he said, his deep gaze and his gentle voice resounding clearly and softly.

I could almost see all the colours of the world pulled into his plain robes, searing their hues into my eyes. All I could do was hold out the shopping bag I'd brought, overwhelmed by the tranquillity of the monk and the old buildings around us.

'Please relax,' the monk said reassuringly. 'I understand.'

Then he was on his feet, and we followed him around to the back of the sanctuary building. There we saw a small glass candle case, a seated Buddha and a large incense burner, the source of the fragrance that enveloped the temple.

The monk handed each of us a stick of incense. 'Go on,' he urged.

We each lit our incense and stuck it in the burner. Two grey plumes wove through the air before dissipating in the breeze.

'Have you ever thought deeply about death?' the monk asked.

'We talked about heart attacks on the way—'

I clapped a hand over Yi-ryeong's mouth. This was a serious question, and I didn't want to offend the monk.

But the monk smiled. 'It is good to be young, to be able to discuss death with such humour,' he said. 'It means that your hearts retain childlike innocence.'

'But we're adults.'

'Childlikeness is not tied to age,' the monk replied, and slowly pulled the objects out of the shopping bag. He placed them on the glass case: the flower-print dress that had clearly been worn, and the grubby basketball. They were both completely out of place.

'When a person dies, they may remain on this earth in spirit form,' said the monk, 'for anywhere between forty-nine days to three years. The shorter their time here, the better – reincarnation is always best, after all.'

Yi-ryeong listened intently, even though she had no context for the monk's explanation. 'You mean the 49th-Day Rite and the Three-Year Mourning?' she asked.

'Indeed. People see them only as traditions now, but there is real meaning behind the rite for the forty-ninth day following death, and the three-year period in which people remember their gratitude and obligations to their late parents. Three years happens to be the amount of time a deceased soul may remain on this earth.'

'What happens if a soul stays longer?'

'Their name is removed from the roster of names to be reborn.'

'You mean the soul is destroyed?'

'No. By the mercy of the Buddha, they are permitted to remain – but as wandering souls, never to find a new life.'

I thought of Mae-hyeon. He'd said he came on the third anniversary of his death. If he'd been any later, he might have never got to reincarnate. 'So someone has to urge these souls to be reborn?' I asked.

The monk turned, his eyes gently narrowed, and nodded. He seemed to know what I'd done and who I'd met.

'But, sir,' I said, 'what if there was someone, say, who died before she got to see her daughter get married? You wouldn't expect her to reincarnate as soon as the forty-nine days had passed. If I were in her shoes, I'd be lingering for three, four years at *least*.'

The monk replied, 'The heavens look graciously upon the virtuous dead, and take away some of their earthly regrets so that they might more easily accept the path to their next life.'

His voice was warm and reassuring, a comforting

embrace that filled the air. In an instant, the nagging doubts in my mind melted away. The woman who'd arrived in the flower-print dress must have moved on peacefully, then. I wasn't so sad anymore.

Looking over the dress and the basketball again, the monk pulled out a small envelope from his robes – inside was enough money to pay for the items, and a hefty sum on top of that.

'What is all this?' I asked.

'You did come for compensation, yes?' the monk asked. 'We've undertaken such transactions for a very long time.'

I couldn't believe it. 'Grandma never told me a thing. She's passed away, you see.'

The monk seemed to have already known that. He placed his hands together and bowed, not for me, but for Grandma. Yi-ryeong backed away and looked around at the temple buildings. I could tell she wanted to give us some space to talk about Grandma.

'The elder monk who once presided over this temple made a request of your ancestor,' the monk explained. 'He had become ill, you see, and could no longer send off the dead as he had once done. And most unfortunately, he was unable to find another monk to follow in his footsteps. That was how your ancestors, in whose blood ran great spiritual powers, began to operate the Hwawoldang. Your family did the work that was meant to be done by this temple, and in exchange, we would compensate them for their services.'

He took the basketball under his arm, but held out the dress.

'You will find good use for this dress later,' he said. 'Keep it.'

'But the owner . . .'

The monk persisted, so I reluctantly took the dress from his hands. I didn't think I'd wear something like that, but what else could I do? Maybe there *was* some unfinished business here.

We clapped our hands before the Buddha. Now I had more information, and the compensation for my work. All I had to do was leave.

Then the monk said, 'You've met Sa-wol, yes?'

I didn't dare try to define the countless emotions in his eyes, old and full of memories.

'The boy is kinder than he lets on,' the monk continued. 'Please don't let appearances deceive you.'

On our way down, we stopped by the bibimbap restaurant Yi-ryeong had spotted earlier. The place wasn't listed on the maps, but everything on the menu *screamed* 'good old-fashioned nature hike'.

'All right,' Yi-ryeong said, taking in the menu. 'Let's get the dotorimuk and the pajeon.'

'Acorn jelly and green onion cake? That calls for makgeolli –'

'I don't mind day drinking –'

'– but I have to open up shop tonight,' I said, shutting her down.

As if on cue, the manager arrived, and took down our orders with an easy smile. 'Are you girls coming from the temple?'

'Yeah, we are.'

'The Buddha must be pleased, getting such young visitors,' she said, and told us that fewer and fewer people were visiting temples now. Then she gave us our hand towels and disappeared into the kitchen with the familiarity of an old neighbour. We opened the window wide, and the ambience of the woods filled our table.

'You talked with the monk about the 49th-Day Rite, right?' Yi-ryeong asked, her brows waggling playfully. 'What was that about?'

I fiddled with my hand towel. 'Not much, he just wanted to tell me stuff about the temple.'

'I could swear there was something going on. Have you been seeing ghosts lately?'

I put down my glass and looked out the window. 'No way.'

'And those weird things you brought – they're from dead people, right?'

'All right.' I put my foot down. 'No more scary stories from you!'

Yi-ryeong went on anyway. 'And that Sa-wol guy he mentioned! Maybe he's a shaman!' She burst into laughter.

She almost startled me more than the ghosts; Yi-ryeong had no idea how right she was. I took a big gulp of water, nearly choked, and retorted, 'He's just a friend who helps out around the shop.'

'Then how does the monk know him?'

'I don't know. Stop asking. It's not important.'

'You don't sound convincing at all.'

'Yi-ryeong, save the detective work for your next Netflix binge.'

She burst into laughter again, reassuring me that she was just making up whatever sounded funny. I laughed along, but a chill ran down my spine. Sometimes, Yi-ryeong's intuition could be scary.

I wondered what she'd say if I told her about the Hwawoldang's real work? It wouldn't change much, but still, I couldn't tell just anyone about it. Sa-wol did say that hidden powers had to remain hidden for them to work. I was sure the dead didn't want their stories becoming local gossip, either.

'Anyway, I hope you get along with him,' Yi-ryeong said.

'Who?'

'That Sa-wol person.'

'What? Why?'

'The monk said he's a good guy, right?' she said, slowly chewing on the kongjaban served on the side. I took a braised bean, too, and rolled it around in the corner of my mouth, but I had so much to think about that I could barely taste the soy sauce.

Yi-ryeong was right – how *did* the monk know Sa-wol? How were they all connected? I finally did have some answers, though, which made me feel a bit better. The Hwawoldang had been sending off the souls of the dead since my ancestors' time, taking objects as payment and handing them to the temple as proof of their work. *So that's how they kept the place afloat all these years.*

That must mean Grandma had worked with Hongseoksa Temple, and knew the monk personally. Did that mean Grandma had met Sa-wol through the temple?

I took a mouthful of kongnamul muchim as I thought of the people in my life. The beansprouts kept their natural blandness, but that struck a lovely balance with the hint of salt in the flavour, like the cook had filled even the side dishes with love. I couldn't wait to dig into the main course.

'Here you are,' the manager said, emerging from the back with a jaw-dropping spread. 'I made sure to add extra for you young things, so eat up!'

The dotorimuk jelly gleamed at the centre of the table, mixed with vinegar and grated cucumber. *Mum and Dad loved dotorimuk too.* I wondered if they'd been reborn as people by now – if they'd forgotten all about me. I bit my lip, hoping Yi-ryeong couldn't see.

The reminders of the people I'd lost were sort of like weekend lunches. They were so ordinary, and happened all the time, but I treasured each of them anyway.

'Excuse me, ma'am,' Yi-ryeong said, pointing at a bottle of makgeolli. 'We didn't order this.'

'It's on the house, ladies.'

'Really? Thank you!'

'Make sure to drop in again, all right?'

Yi-ryeong cheered and filled her makgeolli bowl. As for me? I'd sworn I wouldn't drink before work, but received a bowl anyway.

I was just doing this so I wouldn't cry, I told myself.

'Yeah! Here's to day drinking!'

'Cheers!'

I thought of so many people as I raised my bowl and took that first sip of thick sweetness. As the pleasant tipsiness set in, I reached for the edges of the pajeon, fried almost as crispy as the jeonbyeong crackers, but savoury with the flavour of the oil and the gentle kick of the onion. Then I went for two pieces of the dotorimuk, moist and smooth but supple to chew. The chilli powder, vinegar and sugar offset the hint of acorn bitterness nicely. This combination always reminded me of a certain day in early summer, when I sat in the living room with Grandma and both my parents, eating and talking about nothing in particular.

'Yeon-hwa, you're totally flushed.'

'That's because I'm drunk.'
'You're redder than Hwang Jung-min!'
'I sure am!'

We knocked back bowl after bowl. If grief was as much a part of life as happiness, there was no point trying to escape. That's what being an adult meant: moving forward. That was the future I had to endure.

Thankfully, I wasn't alone.

❀

We hobbled out of the restaurant before the sky was as red as our faces, stinking of makgeolli and hands on each other's shoulders as we danced on our way. The manager didn't frown once as she saw us off.

'No work, lots of drinking, and great company too! Weekends are the best!' Yi-ryeong yelled. She was so happy to finally get away from the daily grind, and insisted we go to karaoke and get ice cream after, just like a drunken middle manager calling for a company hiking trip.

'I have to open up shop now, Yi-ryeong,' I replied.
'Aww, come on! Just take today off.'
'I can't do that.'
Yi-ryeong groaned.

'We'll do all that stuff some other time. What do you say?'

'Fine,' she replied. 'But we have to actually make plans. Not "let's meet up when we're free",' she said, and pulled out her phone, linking her arm with mine. She'd been like this since the last time I got too lazy to make concrete plans with her.

'All right. What do you want to do next time, then?'

'You like art exhibitions, right? I'm going to get tickets *right now*,' Yi-ryeong said flatly.

To be honest, I was so busy learning to run the Hwawoldang that I couldn't make too much time. But I did feel bad about neglecting my friend. 'Okay,' I said, and held up a pinkie finger. 'We'll go next week, how about that?'

Yi-ryeong cheered and sealed the promise. Then she reserved two tickets for the new exhibition at our usual contemporary art museum.

I couldn't not contribute now, not when Yi-ryeong was going out of her way to make sure I wasn't alone. 'Let's pack lunches and eat them outside after the exhibition,' I said.

'Aww, yes!'

Her delighted smile reminded me of the beatific

smiles of the dead as they passed on. Even the smallest pieces of happiness could uplift our hearts. I couldn't do anything by half-measures when something so precious was on the line. I would give my all to my work at the Hwawoldang, and to my friendship with Yi-ryeong.

If the things I said and did could make someone happy, I would make sure to get them right. It felt like that might bring a bit of cheer to Mum, Dad and Grandma, wherever they were now. They would remember me and think, *We're so proud of you, Yeon-hwa.*

4

The Third Customer and the Green Tea Dango

No one showed up for days. Not Sa-wol, not the dead. I told myself it was too hot inside to keep the door shut, but all I did was stare out at the pitch-black sky for days on end, thinking of a perfect stranger who had every right not to show up.

Sa-wol never used the word 'secret', but he *made* secrets with everything he did and said. Did he have a girlfriend? Even that answer was a secret. I didn't mean anything by the question; I was just curious after learning about Seo-hui and Mae-hyeon. But Sa-wol had avoided the question, and now I couldn't stop thinking about it.

That was *far* from the only question Sa-wol didn't answer, though. He still hadn't told me everything about the Hwawoldang and Grandma, which meant I had too many gaps to fill in with my own imagination. He was just like Grandma in that sense.

I wished he would say something.

Then I saw it: a foot through the doorway. I looked up, prepared to see Sa-wol.

'Do you sell dango dumplings here?'

I almost sighed in disappointment. 'Yes,' I told the customer, 'but I'll need to prepare a fresh batch, if you don't mind.'

'I have all the time in the world,' replied the customer, a woman in her late twenties with a conspicuously missing shadow. 'I'm loving the antique vibe in here.'

'Thank you. My grandmother did all this, back when she ran the shop.'

'She had a great eye for interior design, then.'

'I'm sure she would have been happy to hear that.'

The woman seemed to sense that the former owner had gone for good, because she put on a bright smile to cheer me up. She had a big mouth and long eyes, and long brown hair without bangs. A silver heart-shaped pendant hung from her neck, and although her outfit looked simple enough, it was obvious she'd put some thought into it, giving it the kind of lively style that fit right in on a university campus. It was funny to see so much energy in a ghost.

I turned to the recipe booklet, remembering how Grandma had made me dango at home before. Then I found it – and an easy recipe, too. It was even easier now that I'd been practising every day.

'By the way,' the woman said, 'do they also come in green tea flavour?'

'I have matcha powder, if you're all right with that.'

'Great!'

'How many would you like?'

'Let me see,' the woman said, counting her fingers animatedly. Her nails were almost as long as her eyes, and varnished perfectly in beige from root to tip. Her hands looked soft and well-kept too, smooth and tidy all the way around. *She's beautiful*, I thought.

'I thought *I* was the shopper here,' the woman said with a laugh, holding out her hand when she caught me staring.

'Oh, I'm sorry,' I replied, 'I was just distracted. I'm still new to this whole sending-off-the-dead business.'

The woman smiled. 'I can relate to being new.'

I wondered what might have happened to this spirit. What kind of life did she have? Gingerly, I took her hand.

'My name was Kim Jeong-min. I was twenty-eight years old.'

'Right,' I said. 'Please let me look into your memories, Jeong-min.'

'Go right ahead.'

Jeong-min didn't show it, but she appeared eager to get to the point. It seemed like she was used to showing her memories. I closed my eyes again as I dove right into her story.

❁

'Oh no, we're gonna be late!'

An assortment of art supplies were arranged on the living-room floor on a weekend morning as Jeong-min and Su-min rushed to pack everything into their cases.

'Su-min, the size 7 brushes still have paint on them.'

'Crap, I forgot to wash them! I'll pack more of the 6 brushes.'

They had been classmates in art school and were now roommates who shared a forty-square-metre two-bedroom apartment. Today, they were running an art programme for local children at a nearby park. Jeong-min had submitted an impeccable grant proposal to the district office, which would be paying each of them 200,000 won for their work.

If there was one problem, though, it was Su-min's constant mistakes. Jeong-min had to down a whole cup of cold water and take two deep breaths to not lose her patience. 'Slow down, Su-min,' she said. 'Let's go over the supplies list and check one by one—'

'Right, right. So what else did we need?'

'Did you not hear me?'

'What was it now? Right! The water cups!' Su-min cried. She leapt up and rushed across the living room, trampling on a size 6 brush on the way. As the brush snapped, Jeong-min bit her lip and exhaled slowly.

Kim Su-min and Kim Jeong-min had been best friends since they were twenty-two years old. Their names weren't their only similarities: they'd both gone to art school without help from their parents, who'd wanted them to find more promising majors. They were both outgoing and friendly, but secret introverts. They both loved fried chicken and they were both 163 centimetres tall.

Their artistic vision, though, couldn't be more different. Su-min liked to work by hand, and Jeong-min liked digital art. They each finished their visual arts programme with different specialties, so even when they moved in together, they saw each other as trusty sisters-in-arms, not rivals.

'Let's take inventory one more time, Su-min. Are we sure we have everything?'

'We've got brushes, sketchbooks, watercolours, tissues . . . I think we're set to go!'

'Are you sure?'

'Probably?'

'Then we'll check again until we're *certain*.'

Jeong-min was the planner; she was thorough and never overlooked anything, but she tended to worry too much. Su-min was the clumsy improviser, but she was always optimistic. In the six years they'd lived together, they'd learned to make up for each other's weaknesses.

Because today's programme was an offline event for kids, Su-min would have the bigger role to play – which meant Jeong-min had to make sure Su-min didn't make a single mistake.

'I'm done!' Su-min said with a triumphant thumbs-up. 'And this time, I'm *sure* I have everything.'

Jeong-min wasn't feeling too triumphant herself, but they were out of time. She rushed Su-min to the door, where they squeezed their feet into the white buy-one-get-one-free sneakers they'd got together. If this programme went well, the district office might ask them to take on the next one, too. Jeong-min's eyes were locked on her phone all the way down the lift as she ran the numbers in her head.

'That's the utilities for the month, and then subtract the food costs . . .'

'I have a great idea! We should order fried chicken for dinner!'

'. . . then the insurance premiums, and the furnace repairs . . .'

'We can do a half-and-half platter of regular and glazed.'

'That's no good,' Jeong-min said sadly. 'We're spending more than 300,000 on expenses this month – and that's not counting rent.'

Su-min struck a pose straight out of *The Scream*. 'No! My fried chicken!'

Even with two working adults in the household, they always lived hand to mouth.

'Wait, I have another great idea!' Su-min exclaimed. 'Hear me out: we'll skip rent this month!'

'Skip a month of rent for *fried chicken*?'

'Or skip utilities for a month? Would that be easier?'

'I don't believe this, Su-min.'

'We're busting our butts trying to make a living here! We deserve some kind of reward,' Su-min said with a sly grin. But Jeong-min didn't budge. Instead, she held up her phone – and the financial planner app she'd been glued to. They were in the red again this month. Su-min finally deflated.

As they stepped out of the lift, Jeong-min said reassuringly, 'This is all going to pay off at the end of the year, though. Think about what we're working towards.'

'Uh-huh. I'm bouncing with excitement,' Su-min replied gloomily.

'You *will*, once the exhibition opens.'

'That's true.'

They had a good reason for skimping on meals and working themselves to the bone.

Jeong-min and Su-min had always wanted to hold solo exhibitions after graduation, but they'd never been able to afford it. This year, though, would be different. They would rent out gallery space to hold a joint exhibition in December. For once in their lives, they would spare no expense. The rental, the transport and the cost of materials would be significant, but it was still *just* painfully affordable for them if they resolved to live the rest of the year in poverty.

'Let's keep our chin up, Su-min. We have to do this while we still have—'

'While we still have time, I know. And I know what you're going to say after that, too.'

'Yeah?'

'Uh-huh,' Su-min said, and then, as though having read each other's minds, they said in unison:

'Time is money! So save it and work real hard!'

Life was never easy, but they had each other. They could get through anything. Even the weather was on their side that day, with the sun just warm enough to be balmy. The foliage over the fence was lush and vibrant, too. Although the pavement was almost too narrow for them to walk side by side, and the city towered over their heads, they felt like they were strolling through a lovely open field, their supplies in hand.

Even though they lived in the same house, Jeong-min and Su-min never seemed to run out of things to talk about. They discussed the dog they saw across the road, the older students from their school days, and more. They never got bored, and although they didn't have many friends other than each other, loneliness never could seem to get a foothold between them.

'I bet we'll have a big turnout today.'

'Thirty kids signed up, I hear.'

'We're going to get crushed today, aren't we?'

Children in groups of threes or fours waited under the large canopy that had been set up in the park. Su-min and Jeong-min felt like a pair of hens wrangling their chicks, with Jeong-min drawing on her years of experience to get their attention and introduce the programme, while Su-min quickly set up their workstations. Before they knew it, they'd got the kids focused on their watercolours. One child painted a maple tree that wasn't there, while another child painted a poorly shaped adult they claimed was their mother, and another rendered a passing cat.

'Su-min, I spilled my water.'

'I'll be right there.'

Su-min swept and mopped and tidied as the kids went on, making sure they had the best time and didn't bother each other too much.

'Jeong-min, how do I do the sun?'

'You can try painting a yellow circle –'

'But it's so bright. How do you *know* it's a circle?'

Jeong-min was in charge of cleaning the other

half as she instructed the kids, who were bottomless wells of questions. *What's this, Jeong-min? What's this thing he drew?* Su-min and Jeong-min were about to faint with exhaustion, but they couldn't afford to collapse now.

Forty minutes later, the kids were finishing up their work, and their parents came to the park to pick them up. Su-min and Jeong-min made sure to clap for every child who finished a watercolour. The kids were tiring, but they were also cuter than puppies when they got some praise.

But one of the children did *not* go home hand-in-hand with a parent. A girl.

'Is everything all right?' Su-min asked. 'Are you having some trouble with your painting?'

'No.'

'. . . Wow! What a nice picture. Is this you and your grandma?'

'Yeah, it's a family portrait.'

Jeong-min joined them, and Su-min whispered to her that the girl's grandmother hadn't come to get her yet. They couldn't start putting the table away until the girl left, but Jeong-min didn't send her away. Su-min bent down and kept talking to the girl so she wouldn't feel left out.

'Hey, what's this little shape between you and your grandma?'

'He's our cat.'

'Oh! Then let me show you how to draw a cat,' Su-min offered, and painted a cat's face on another piece of paper. The girl quickly mimicked Su-min, and soon she had a complete family portrait with a proper cat between the humans. She cheered, and Su-min ran an affectionate hand over her head. 'Painting's not always easy, but don't you ever give up, okay?' she said. 'Art is honest. You improve exactly as much as you practice.'

'Okay!'

The girl beamed, but Su-min couldn't help doubting herself. She and Jeong-min knew better than anyone just how little effort could matter in the world of art. They were both twenty-eight and talented, and yet they struggled to find even one-off jobs as artists. Art was *not* always honest.

It wasn't long before the girl's grandmother arrived. 'I am so sorry!' she exclaimed guiltily, realizing that all of the other kids had gone home already. 'I was just getting some shopping done. Thank you for taking care of my granddaughter.' Then she held out a plastic bag. 'Here, consider it a late fee.'

'We're all right, ma'am. There's no need for that.'

But the old woman wouldn't take no for an answer. 'Please, it wasn't much at all. I insist.'

Inside the plastic bag was a roast chicken from the local market. Su-min refused politely exactly once, and then took the chicken without another thought. The old woman thanked them again and again for watching her granddaughter before she left. The girl never stopped smiling.

They tidied up later than they'd expected, wiping away spilled watercolours and picking up garbage. The aroma of roast chicken seemed to seduce them from the plastic bag, but they had to finish clearing their corner of the park. Su-min gulped.

Fortunately, clean-up didn't take long.

'So, Su-min, what was that girl painting?'

'Her family.'

'Most kids paint their families, huh.'

'I bet most adults would too.'

The supplies felt heavier than they had in the morning, but they left the park with an accomplished spring in their steps.

❦

Su-min's nostrils flared as she took in the smell of the roast chicken. 'This is *destiny*, Jeong-min!' she declared. 'And you know what a chicken party needs? A decent dessert! Otherwise we're going straight to hell!'

'. . . Probably not, but we can get something cheap,' Jeong-min conceded.

'Sun-yeong Tteok it is, then!'

It was mid-afternoon, and their backs were sweaty with the weight of their packs. But they didn't care. They talked about the exact same things they'd talked about on their way to the park, because they never ran out of things to say.

Sun-yeong Tteok was the only dessert shop near their apartment. Rice cakes were a little old-fashioned compared to the western desserts their peers liked, but they were cheaper, and came in a lot of varieties. Named after the owner's daughter, Sun-yeong Tteok had a no-frills name and no-frills rice cakes that all the locals loved. Jeong-min and Su-min's favourite item at Sun-yeong's was the dango.

'Look, look,' Jeong-min said. 'They have new flavours.'

'Let's try the green tea! It's only 3,000 a pack. What a steal!'

Jeong-min picked up the pack of green tea dango, which was only a thousand won more expensive than their usual soy sauce dango.

Her phone buzzed with a text message.

URGENT: Issue Concerning Gallery Space Rental Deposit

Dear Ms Kim Jeong-min,

This is the Gold Gallery. There seems to have been a mistake concerning your deposit for the gallery space rental this December. The end of the year is considered our busy season, and the deposit for this time is higher than the rest of the year. Your recent deposit was only equivalent to the amount charged for the off-season. We request that the difference be paid as soon as possible in order to secure your . . .

Jeong-min froze. She quickly went to the contract she'd e-signed, and realized that the message was right. The Gold Gallery had two different rates, and she confirmed that their joint exhibition fell during the busy season. Even Jeong-min made mistakes sometimes, and this time, her mistake meant they were short 400,000 on the all-important deposit.

The exact amount they'd made that day.

'What's up, Jeong-min?' Su-min asked. 'You look like someone just died.'

'We paid the wrong amount for the Gold Gallery rental deposit.'

'By how much?'

'Four hundred thousand.'

'What?' Su-min exclaimed. 'That's our pay for today.'

Jeong-min sighed. 'There's not much we can do. I'll pay the difference now.'

'Or – or maybe we could forget the Gold Gallery. There's plenty of small exhibition spaces in the suburbs.'

The Gold Gallery was in a busy district of Seoul with heavy local foot traffic – which meant young visitors were regulars there, which in turn meant that exhibitions at the Gold Gallery were more likely to get big buzz. Rumour had it that the best art agencies in the country dropped in regularly to scout promising young artists. Jeong-min and Su-min were in their late twenties now, and still completely unknown. They'd been looking for this chance for years. The Gold Gallery exhibition was their biggest, and maybe their final, shot at making a name for themselves in the industry.

But like most unknown artists, they had doubts. Sometimes they felt like an underground rock band holding a concert at a 15,000-seat stadium. They would get *prestige*, but no one could promise that people would actually come to see them. What if they were aiming too high?

'We can't stop now,' Jeong-min said. 'I'd rather regret reaching for the stars than not trying at all. We can get the green tea dango some other time.'

'Too bad.'

The 3,000-won dango pack went back to the shelf, relegated to some undefined time in their future. If Jeong-min had her way, they wouldn't bring home any dango at all – but they had a happiness quota to fill that day, and chose to enjoy their usual dose of delight instead. Jeong-min and Su-min weren't prim or tight-fisted – they knew how to compromise sometimes.

Once they'd both taken showers, they spread the two-person table in the living room and set the roast chicken in the middle, now just cool enough to wolf down. Jeong-min tore open the small pack of pickled radishes that came with the chicken and crunched as she planned for tomorrow.

'I have a class to teach on Monday, and then

commissions after that. Could you help me with the colouring?'

'Sure,' Su-min replied. 'It's been a while since I touched a tablet.'

'You should pick it back up again. There's so much demand for digital art.'

'I just can't get the hang of it.'

'Think about the money, Su-min.'

'The things we do for cash,' Su-min groaned. 'Sometimes you're worse than my mum.' She felt a headache coming on. Having something to motivate her was a good thing, but she never enjoyed remembering her stress. 'Ugh, did I not chew properly?' she wondered, putting down a drumstick and pounding at her chest. 'I feel sick.'

'Oh no, not again,' Jeong-min said, as Su-min rushed to the bathroom and bent over the toilet. Jeong-min quickly tidied the table and dug up medication. Then she waited outside the bathroom door like a dog waiting for its master.

Su-min had been throwing up so often it was worrying. It happened more when she was discussing uncomfortable subjects. She also had trouble sleeping when she had to help out with digital-art commissions. Jeong-min felt guilty, as if she was being greedy to the point of making Su-min sick.

The things that made Su-min ill were all painfully clear, and painfully unavoidable: thoughts of work, money and the future. So Jeong-min tried not to talk about those things over food, but it was so easy to forget, especially on days like today.

It's all my fault, she thought, ashamed of always being so occupied with work and money. She wished she'd keep those worries to herself, instead of burdening her best and only friend with all the stress.

'Ugh,' Su-min groaned as she emerged from the bathroom, having rinsed out her mouth.

Jeong-min handed Su-min an antacid and asked, 'Have you thought about getting a check-up?'

'They cost too much.'

'But you keep getting nauseous. What if there's a problem?'

'You do have a point . . .'

'See? We might be poor, but we'd be stupid to get sick just to save a bit of money. Let's get you checked out soon,' Jeong-min said, and immediately pulled out her phone. The local hospital charged a base fee of 100,000 won for a basic check-up and stomach ulcer tests.

Su-min frowned. 'That's too much.'

'One hundred thousand should be doable.'

'No, it's going to cost at least 200,000.'

'Why?'

'You need a check-up too. We're saving up together; we can't spend that much on me and not on you.'

'*My* stomach is fine, Su-min,' Jeong-min insisted, opening up the pack of dango and taking one skewer. She tore off each ball of dough with her teeth. The sweetness quickly gave way to a salty aftertaste – the perfect end to any meal. 'See? No problems here.'

'Hey!' Su-min complained. 'Leave the other two for me.'

'Nope. You're not getting any this time.'

'Why not?'

'No desserts until your check-up.'

Their conversation was quickly forgotten as Su-min and Jeong-min bantered over the rest of the dango. They rode out the waves of misfortune as they came, never thinking to give up. They were the sisters they'd never had, and because they rarely spoke with their respective parents, who weren't well-off enough to help, they saw each other as family – people they put before themselves, even though they weren't related by blood. People they hoped to succeed with.

'I'm going to book you the first slot I can find. And don't worry about the colouring; I can find an assistant.'

'... All right,' Su-min finally said. 'I'll get checked out, okay?'

They hoped each day that the other would be healthy, that the other would not suffer. They cared for each other as much as – if not more than – themselves. They were rich at heart, which meant poverty could never make them lonely.

♣

Su-min's diagnosis was a gastric polyp. It didn't sound too serious, but the polyp had progressed to the point that the doctor recommended hospitalization and surgery.

When Su-min rushed to call her parents to ask about her health insurance, her parents replied that they had cancelled the policy because they simply couldn't afford it. Su-min hadn't got herself insured since she was sure she was still young and healthy. She would have to pay the entirety of her medical fees out of her own pocket.

'Maybe I can push back the treatment,' she wondered. 'It's just a bit of puking. I don't think I need *surgery* for that.'

But Jeong-min wouldn't take no for an answer. She *couldn't* put off the operation. It was almost frustrating sometimes how they took better care of each other than themselves. 'No working until you've recovered,' Jeong-min added.

'But what about all the work we already have?'

'I can do it myself.'

'You're already doing so much –'

'I can handle it.'

While Su-min rested, Jeong-min took over all her shifts at the extracurricular art classes. Thankfully, her students were understanding, and the work wasn't as hard as she'd expected. When she got home, Jeong-min did her usual commissions – but not with an assistant, although she'd told Su-min she had one. An assistant cost too much, so she would work until four in the morning regularly to make her deadlines.

I'm glad it's not taking too much effort to get enough done, Su-min thought.

Fortunately, or unfortunately, Jeong-min managed. She went to bed at four in the morning and woke up at nine to get to work. Su-min, meanwhile, rested so she would be in good condition for her upcoming surgery. But her passion for art couldn't be beaten by a bit of nausea, even if the stress of it had caused the sickness in the first place.

'I can go back to teaching now. I'm feeling a lot better.'

'Not until your surgery,' Jeong-min said firmly. She pushed Su-min back into bed and covered her with a blanket. 'You're not allowed to work until you're healthy.'

'But what about living expenses?'

'I'm getting paid for the commission soon.'

'But you have to pay the assistant –'

Su-min couldn't finish her sentence. She heaved again. Jeong-min quickly handed her a tissue, but Su-min was already running to the bathroom. While she coughed up the rice porridge she'd had for breakfast, Jeong-min watched with concern, almost about to cry.

When Su-min looked up, there was blood on her lip. But she tried to hide it and smiled. 'I just need to rinse out my mouth,' she argued, and told Jeong-min to go back to her room, but Jeong-min couldn't bear to leave her alone.

They stood with the doorway between them, each filled with guilt. It was as bitter and sticky as badly made dango.

●

The operation was a resounding success.

The doctor recommended two days of hospitalization. Su-min protested, but such a short stay wouldn't cost much, Jeong-min thought. She insisted that Su-min follow the doctor's orders.

Su-min lay in a daze in her hospital bed, wearing a hospital gown for the first time in her life. The whole time, she made ridiculous promises.

'Once I'm out of here, I'll do three times as much work as usual.'

'We don't get that much work, Su-min.'

'Then two-point-five times as much.'

Jeong-min stayed at Su-min's side at the hospital, still doing commission work on her tablet. She hadn't mentioned to Su-min that she'd taken on another job and the deadline was just around the corner. It was hard to pretend not to be extremely busy.

'What do you want to eat when you're out of here?'

'Hm, let's see . . . dango!'

'Then we'll get some as soon as you're out.'

'I can't wait!'

A stick of dango was nothing. Jeong-min swore that she'd pick up the green tea flavour this time as she focused on her art. Their conversations weren't productive or urgent, but somehow they seemed to wash away their guilt. Jeong-min made sure to smile brightly for Su-min to see even as her right hand moved endlessly over her screen.

'You're going to teach my class tonight, right?' Su-min asked. 'You should go home and rest afterwards. I'll be fine on my own.'

'Are you sure?'

'Positive.'

Su-min made Jeong-min promise to get a proper dinner – 'Because I can't!' – and Jeong-min nodded half-heartedly as she left the hospital. She didn't have *time* for food, but that wasn't a bad thing, because she would spend less money. One missed meal was nothing compared to what Su-min had suffered, and Jeong-min would feel bad if she feasted while Su-min recovered in hospital without anything to eat.

When her mother died, Jeong-min's father had told her, 'Now you have to learn to take care of yourself and others.' He meant that he could no longer afford to support her creative work, and that she would need to contribute to the household as one of its pillars. Jeong-min had nodded without a second thought.

Now it's my turn to take care of someone else.

Jeong-min was responsible by nature. That nature became her biggest problem.

She headed straight from the hospital to Su-min's art class. Things seemed to go well at first, but Jeong-min found herself sniffling, and one of the students looked up in shock.

'Jeong-min, you're bleeding.'

Drops of blood spattered onto the corner of the student's paper. 'Sorry, let me get you a new one,' Jeong-min said, and wadded up some tissue to stuff into the offending nostril before picking up fresh paper. She didn't *want* to know her own condition. She'd been exhausted recently, and had more headaches than usual, but thinking about that made it hard to focus. A nosebleed was nothing compared to a gastric polyp, and she wanted to keep thinking optimistically for her mental health, too. Jeong-min took a painkiller to prevent any headaches from coming on.

'Jeong-min, were you thinking of something nasty? That's when people get nosebleeds, right?'

'Hee hee! You were thinking something naughty, Jeong-min!'

The students' worry quickly turned to good-natured teasing, and Jeong-min loved them for it. But she wouldn't let comments like that slide. 'Min-ji and So-yeon, you're both getting thirty minutes of detention today. Prepare to paint some more.'

Min-ji and So-yeon screamed, and for a moment, Jeong-min forgot all her troubles. She had to change the tissue in her nostril three or four times before the class ended, but nothing could stop her. She had art to create, students to teach, and a best friend to care for.

❀

When Su-min was discharged, the doctor warned Jeong-min that Su-min would have to watch her diet now. Gastric polyps had a high recurrence rate; in the worst-case scenario, she could develop stomach cancer.

As they walked stiffly out the doors, Su-min said, 'I guess that's it for fried chicken, then.'

'Yeah, but only for now.'

'So what *do* I get to eat?'

'Cabbage soup, pickled cabbage, cabbage ssam, doenjangguk soup with cabbage . . .'

'What am I, a rabbit?' Su-min waved her hands in frustration. Her wrists were almost bony now. Jeong-min knew she'd have to feed Su-min as much cabbage as she could to get her back to a healthy weight. She quietly added more heads of cabbage to her grocery delivery order.

Before they knew it, they were at Sun-yeong Tteok. It was time to keep her promise.

'Let's celebrate with green tea dango,' Jeong-min proposed, because this would be the only treat Su-min could have before she started her all-cabbage diet.

But Su-min caught her hand before she could grab the pack of dango. 'Actually, I want the soy sauce flavour today,' she said.

'But why?'

'I'm craving something salty.'

'You've been talking about the green tea flavour for *days*,' Jeong-min said, noticing a strangely serious look in Su-min's eyes. 'If this is about the money, don't worry about it,' she insisted. 'It's only a thousand won.'

'I just want the soy sauce flavour, okay? I mean it, Jeong-min.'

Jeong-min didn't know what to make of her best friend's change of heart, but couldn't argue now.

The truth was, Su-min had seen Jeong-min's wrist, too. She'd spotted a small, skin-tone cooling patch on her right wrist, which could only mean she'd been working so hard that it ached. She still wanted to try the green tea dango someday, and 1,000 won was pocket change, but she couldn't bring herself to act like a spoiled child now. *Jeong-min's had it rough because of me*, she thought. She wanted to be Jeong-min's friend, not a burden to carry.

❀

As Su-min recovered, she slowly took on more and more of her usual work. Soon they were saving together for the joint exhibition again. And this time, nothing could stop them. Jeong-min and Su-min faced each day head-on, tossing back painkillers and antacids as they worked gruelling hours for what seemed like an eternity.

By early July, however, their routine had to change. They stopped taking commissions and did exactly enough work to pay the bills and put food on the table. It was time to prepare for the December exhibition, where they would showcase contemporary visual reimaginings of Korean folktales under the theme of 'East Asian Legends Re-Interpreted'. But although this was a joint exhibition, they would each draw inspiration from different references so they could showcase their individual strengths and talents. After renting a small half-basement unit as a temporary workspace and moving their supplies over, they set up their respective tables and got to work.

'Did you pick a story yet?' Su-min asked, chewing on a gummy as she came by Jeong-min's workstation.

Jeong-min nodded. 'Yeah, I'm thinking about the Legend of the Red Boulder.'

'Never heard of that one, but it sounds dramatic.'

'Right? It's from the Joseon era. A blind old man was travelling up a mountain by himself, when a boulder nearby caught on fire. The old man felt the heat from the flames and put out the fire with all his strength, but he was burned badly all over. But the boulder god thanked the old man and gave him a great reward.'

'What'd he get?'

'The ability to see spirits,' Jeong-min explained.

'And that power was passed down through his descendants, who used the ability to bring peace to people.'

'So it's like a hero myth, huh? That's pretty cool.'

'You know what's even cooler? The burnt boulder is supposed to be around even now. The people who got help from the old man's family built a Buddhist temple by the rock.'

'What's the temple called?'

Jeong-min shuffled through her books and files, which were all about the red boulder. But none of her sources mentioned the temple's name. 'Oh well,' she finally said. 'It's not really important.'

'True,' Su-min agreed, and as Jeong-min tidied up her things, Su-min placed her bundle of references on her desk. 'Check this out. Mine's a bit of a scary one.'

'Ooh, a horror story?'

'Ever heard about the Rule of Soul Exchanges?'

'No.'

'If you save a life that was supposed to end, another person has to lose their life. That's why you're not supposed to intervene with people's destiny –'

'That's terrible! In a good way, I mean. Do you think you can do this?'

'Of course I can,' Su-min said with a proud grin, holding out an eerie reference picture. 'I can't wait. We'd better get tons of visitors!'

Jeong-min smiled. 'We will.'

'If we hit it big and make a lot of money, what's the first thing you want to do?'

'Hm,' Jeong-min intoned, and fell into thought. 'I guess . . . I just want to live like everyone else.'

Soon, breaktime was over, and Jeong-min and Su-min were each at their desks again. They didn't have any windows, but what did that matter? They didn't need to see the sun or moon when a bright fluorescent light shone over them all day round. And they had each other. When they were hungry or tired, they could lean on one another for support. Sometimes they'd see updates from successful classmates on social media, and fall into self-pity. Jeong-min clung to little rays of hope each day, like the prospect of getting nice nail art done like her richer friends. Filling her brush with those dreams, she pressed on. The speakers never stopped playing their favourite songs, alternating between playlists.

Their work went smoothly. Before long, both Jeong-min and Su-min had multiple works to fill the Gold Gallery's exhibition hall, and they'd each planned out layouts and paths. All they needed now was some sort of link to connect their respective showcases.

It was the start of autumn when Jeong-min discovered that their savings were almost gone. They'd been too busy with art to think about money, and now she found herself strategizing again. *Do I cut down on food costs? Materials? Where can I cut spending?* It was like a hole had opened up in their finances, draining the money as it came in.

'Big news, Jeong-min!' Su-min cried, bursting into the workshop. 'The Gold Foundation people are coming to see the exhibition.'

'What? But we haven't done any promo work.'

'Remember Eun-hui? She's an intern at the foundation, and she showed them our portfolios. Now they want to see our work in person!'

The Gold Foundation was a generous patron of up-and-coming artists. They provided massive grants each year, introduced new talent to all sorts of collaborative opportunities, and hosted networking events with established artists to foster the next generation of creators. Unfortunately, they were as picky as they were open-handed. The Gold Foundation rarely responded to portfolio submissions and didn't respond to exhibition invitations even from the most popular artists in the industry.

This was a Golden opportunity.

Even if the foundation didn't choose to support them, the fact that they'd visited at all would help their work go viral, drawing other potential patrons.

'What's wrong, Jeong-min?'

Jeong-min could not say a word.

'Hey, are you crying?'

Her eyes were red. For once in her life, she was not calm.

'It's okay, Jeong-min,' Su-min said, pulling her into a powerful hug and almost sobbing herself. But as she wiped away tears of joy, she frowned. 'Hey, your nose is bleeding.'

Jeong-min gave a casual grin and stuffed tissue into her nostril. Nothing could dampen her spirits now.

Su-min, though, seemed worried. 'You must be tired. Maybe you should go for a check-up yourself.'

'It's just a nosebleed,' Jeong-min replied with the biggest smile in the world. Now Su-min couldn't bring herself to point out how pale Jeong-min had got recently. They were both fighting exhaustion each day to prepare for the biggest event of their lives, and Su-min knew that the road to December wouldn't be easy.

Jeong-min could sense the warm encouragement in her gaze.

❀

As October entered full swing, Jeong-min finally decided to see a doctor about her frequent nosebleeds.

'I can't see anything especially worrying in your nose,' the doctor said after the exam. Most chronic nosebleeds happened because of dry mucus membranes or fragile blood vessels in the nostrils, but Jeong-min's nose seemed perfectly fine. 'How often do these episodes occur?'

'Almost every other day, recently.'

'That's very frequent.'

'I think I must be working too hard,' Jeong-min said dismissively.

But the doctor had a different hunch. 'I wouldn't say that, necessarily. The nose doesn't respond directly to levels of fatigue. The bleeding must have a different cause – it's rare, but it might be related to the sensory nerves. I'll refer you to a specialist for a comprehensive exam. Please, do *not* ignore this issue.'

But Jeong-min only gave a half-hearted nod as she rose.

The doctor said firmly, 'The sensory *nerves* aren't controlled by sensory *organs*, do you understand? This could be a more serious issue.'

Jeong-min, though, only nodded again. She regretted spending the money on a check-up that went nowhere. *What's my nose matter? I'm happy as long as my hand still works.* It was a tiny price to pay, she thought. The ability to smell had nothing to do with her work. She didn't need to smell and taste clearly to make it big as an artist. This could wait until after the exhibition.

Once she'd paid at the desk, she was given a referral to a specialist, and to a large hospital where she could get a comprehensive check-up. 'How much would that cost?' she asked.

'About 150,000 won for a CT scan.'

'Right. Thank you.'

Jeong-min had to hold back a snort. Part of her had thought about getting the exam, but 150,000 won was out of the question when she had materials to buy and prints to have transported.

As she headed home, she examined the doctor's referral again.

'A CT scan,' she said in disbelief. 'That's just how hospitals make money off people.'

It felt good, knowing she'd just saved 150,000 won – which was almost the same as *making* 150,000 won. Jeong-min decided that all she needed to do was stress less, and practically skipped on her way.

Then she spotted a flea market in the park by the subway station. And one of the first tables caught her eye.

20,000-won Friendship Lockets: Buy 1, Get 1 Free!

The handmade lockets were shaped like hearts, with space for a photo inside and a shiny silver cover. Jeong-min remembered taking a four-cut photo with Su-min a few months ago, and imagined putting matching pictures into a pair of matching lockets.

'That's it!'

Her eyes flew open. She knew how to tie their exhibitions together.

❀

By November, they were installing partitions and completing the layout of the gallery space. Jeong-min and Su-min almost squealed as they brought their dreams to life. They couldn't afford to hire help, but they had all the skills they needed to realize a polished exhibition. The gallery manager dropped in often to check on their progress.

'It's interesting having two artists holding a joint exhibition on a single theme,' she remarked. 'But right now, the two sections do feel a bit disconnected.'

Jeong-min and Su-min had to agree. They'd given each other total artistic freedom, so their respective works weren't cohesive at all. The manager's comment hit on the problem they'd been struggling with for months.

But just as Su-min deflated, Jeong-min looked the manager confidently in the eye. 'We have an idea for that.'

'Really? Will you be implementing it soon?'

'Yes, very soon,' Jeong-min replied.

The manager promised to come back once the adjoining element was ready, and left with an encouraging word. Meanwhile, Su-min gave Jeong-min a quizzical look.

Jeong-min pulled two lockets out of her pocket. 'Here. Open them up.'

Inside each locket was a cutout of a picture of them together.

'This is adorable!' Su-min exclaimed. 'I had no idea you were working on this.'

Smiling, Jeong-min explained, 'These pendants are all we need to tie our exhibitions together. You and me, we look similar, we have similar names, and we've been best friends for years – but our art styles are completely different. I'm going to display these pendants right in the middle of the space, so people can use our friendship as a reference point for interpreting the connection between our work.'

They would set up a pair of plaster torsos in the middle of the gallery, Jeong-min explained. The torsos would face each other, and each would be wearing one locket.

'Then we can put the one with my locket in front of your section, and the one with your locket in front of my section,' Su-min suggested. 'I bet that'll be even more evocative.'

'That sounds great!'

'Hey, can I wear this locket until we have to use it for the exhibition?'

'Sure.'

Su-min was delighted. Whatever the lockets might have cost, it was worth the world to her. Jeong-min felt like Su-min's smile was enough – and more – to make up for the money she'd spent on them. Together, they strolled through the still-empty gallery space and chatted excitedly about December.

'You know what?' said Su-min. 'We should do another one if this one goes well.'

Su-min was never afraid to talk about the future, because with someone as careful as Jeong-min by her side, she could happily hold nothing but joint exhibitions for the rest of her life. She put herself into a visitor's shoes as she headed for the exit, Jeong-min following behind her.

'We get along so well,' Su-min went on, her voice a song that filled the gallery. She pictured their works all across the walls and partitions to either side, thinking of their dreams becoming reality. 'It's like we're always on the same wavelength.'

She loved daydreaming about their exhibitions gaining popularity, and becoming a celebrated artist. About a life where she didn't need to take commissions, didn't get hounded by clients left and right. She knew she shouldn't count her chickens before they hatched, but today, she could make an exception. She wanted to always look forward to tomorrow, to always be excited for the future. Hopefully, with Jeong-min at her side.

Once they had more money, they could go on holiday overseas. They could visit the Louvre and the Museo del Prado. They could eat good food and wear nice clothes. Su-min had no end of heart-pounding dreams, each of them featuring both herself and Jeong-min.

'I bet we were twins in our past life! Or maybe doppelgangers!'

She turned.

There was a thud, and Su-min's doppelganger collapsed to the floor.

❀

The last thing I saw in Jeong-min's life was the image of her best friend, marching energetically ahead. Then the world seemed to go off-kilter, and everything went dark. These were Jeong-min's final moments.

I let go of her. 'What happened?'

Jeong-min held up her hand and looked at her fingernails, closing her hand into a fist and opening it again. It was like she was remembering the warmth of a living person.

There was no sorrow in her face. The monk was right, then – the dead really didn't have the regrets they had in life. But that only made Jeong-min look like she'd lost half her emotions.

'It was a brain tumour,' she said.

'But how could you not notice something so serious?' I asked.

Jeong-min shrugged. 'I can't say I didn't notice. The warning signs were there, and I ignored them.'

'But it was so sudden.'

'Yes, but only because I dismissed the nosebleeds and the headaches,' Jeong-min replied, and turned. She looked out at the night sky wistfully. 'If I'd known it would end so soon, I'd have at least tried the green tea dango,' she said in a joking tone, but my heart ached.

Grandma had been dismissive about her health, too. She didn't go to the doctor much, and she always went alone. When I asked if she was sick, she'd just hold up her medication and tell me not to worry, because she was taking good care of herself. I assumed all old people got sick like she did. But death was a silent customer. Light and invisible as air, until it finally struck.

'You make sure to take care of yourself,' Jeong-min said. 'Don't put off your dreams like I did. Just look at my nails.'

'I . . . um . . . thank you for that advice, I guess.'

'Anyway, can you make me some green tea dango?'

It was my turn now. I opened up the recipe booklet and found the instructions for the soy sauce flavour, but this wouldn't be as simple as substituting soy sauce for matcha powder.

'There's no rush,' Jeong-min said serenely.

'It's all right, I can do this before midnight –'

'I don't know about the other customers, but I'll be all right.'

I didn't understand how she could be so calm. Time was running out.

'I'd love to chat while I wait. Please, take your time.'

'. . . All right,' I relented, hoping this *was* all right.

As I went to the kitchen, Jeong-min said, 'Tell me about your other customers. What were they reborn as?'

'I've never seen them be reincarnated,' I said, kneading the glutinous rice powder. 'They leave the Hwawoldang, and I never see them again.' Once the dough was ready, I got to work on the sweet and sticky mitarashi sauce. It was made of sugar boiled down in soy sauce, but for this variation, I used a lot less soy sauce and added green tea powder instead.

The sauce wasn't as salty, and had a more bitter flavour. Once the balled dough had been steamed to perfection, I skewered and ladled sauce over them.

Finally, I placed the skewers of dango in a clear plastic container. They looked good enough to sell – and were almost identical to the packs of dango Jeong-min had always wanted to get for Su-min, that Su-min had turned down out of guilt. Their love and consideration had been reborn into little green orbs of bitter dough.

'Your green tea dango,' I said, holding out one skewer I hadn't put into the plastic packaging.

Jeong-min replied, 'They're beautiful,' and ate one dango straight off the skewer. The dango seemed more watery than sticky, so I watched anxiously as she slowly chewed.

'. . . Is the dango all right? Was there something inside?'

'No, well . . .'

I quickly looked over the unpacked dango. Everything *looked* right.

Meanwhile, Jeong-min went on chewing and finally answered, 'I've never had green tea dango before, and . . .'

'. . . And? Is it good?'

'No, it's horrible!' she exclaimed, putting down the skewer with a shake of the head. But there was a big smile on her face. 'I think I prefer the soy sauce flavour. I can't stand the bitter stuff. Honestly, why was Su-min so obsessed with something like this?'

'. . . Oh.' I sighed. 'But I worked so hard on it.'

Jeong-min said, 'Don't take it the wrong way. You did a great job. I'm happy that I finally know what this tastes like. I just wish Su-min could have seen me cringe.' Then, she seemed to deflate. 'Could I ask you a favour?'

'Let me guess,' I said. 'A delivery?'

'Yes. Please get these dango to Su-min. I've been waiting for this day for so long. You know, Ms Manager? Sometimes, waiting is the perfect form of love.'

'Wait, what –'

Then a speck of dust got in my eye, and I quickly tried to rub it away – and she was gone. Only the glass door gaped open, the bell still ringing. I wondered if this was what a haunting felt like.

On the table, I found a ticket to an art exhibition, and a locket.

I'd never really liked the word 'waiting'.

❀

The exhibition ticket happened to be for the exact one Yi-ryeong had got us on the day of the hike. And it was for an artist called 'Su-min'. I wondered if this was fate or coincidence, and tried to take it in my stride.

Early the next morning, I got bad news from Yi-ryeong.

'Sorry, Yeon-hwa. I have to go to work this weekend for some new project component.'

'What about the exhibition?'

'I'm not getting out until evening. You should go without me.'

Because tickets were sold for specific dates, the gallery couldn't give Yi-ryeong an exchange. All she could do was get a refund, and after a round of cursing her employer, apologize profusely to me.

'Hey, I have a great idea,' she said suddenly. 'You should ask that guy to go with you.'

'Who?'

'O-wol.'

'You mean Sa-wol?'

'April, May, what's the difference? Either way, springtime's the prettiest season,' she joked.

So on Saturday afternoon, I found myself standing side by side at the gallery with Sa-wol. I would have been happy to go alone, but I did have two tickets – my e-ticket and the physical one from Jeong-min – and a ticket from the dead could spread dark energies if it went to a normal person like Yi-ryeong. Sa-wol was the perfect companion for the visit, in that sense.

'I'm a busy man,' he'd said. 'And getting called out on a weekend for a free gallery visit sounds great to me.'

'I can't tell if you're happy or upset.'

'I can't say no to free tickets.'

Dressed in a yellow button-down shirt and a pair of jeans, he looked nothing like a shaman today. Sa-wol stretched, his long arms almost reaching the sky. He hummed all the way, happy to finally take a break from the daily grind – whatever that meant for a shaman supplier of ingredients – and took in the breeze. It made him a little cute for his height. I couldn't believe I was worried he'd turn down the invitation.

'Let's grab a taxi to the gallery,' I said, taking out my phone.

Sa-wol stopped me. 'I'd rather not.'

'But it's not going to be expensive. I'm paying.'

'We're *walking*.'

Sa-wol insisted on hoofing it to the gallery, and

no matter how much I explained that it was my treat, he kept changing the subject.

'So the ghost gave you my ticket?' he confirmed. 'And we have to deliver this pack of green tea dango to the artist there?'

'That's right. She's going to be in today.'

Sa-wol asked about the dango recipe, and then about the other treats I'd been learning to make. But every time I felt like I was getting to know him better, he seemed to pull away.

I wanted to ask him about everything I'd heard at the temple. But he went on talking about the Hwawoldang and traditional desserts, and wouldn't let me get a word in. I only forgave him because he looked so *genuine* when he smiled like that. *Oh well. Let's not put a damper on his mood this time.*

A long vertical screen at the gallery entrance displayed information about the exhibition. Sa-wol stuck his hands in his pockets and read it out loud. '*Rising East Asian artist Kim Su-min's first solo exhibition. "Memorial", a dedication to eternal recollections featuring the works of a fallen star . . .* Sounds meaningful.'

'I guess she's featuring another artist's final works, too.'

We showed our tickets at the counter and took in the exhibition space. The gallery was vast, and displayed traditional East Asian artworks featuring auspicious symbols like tigers, cranes, the sun and moon, and natural landscapes. However, the work was digital, and coloured in a contemporary style. I couldn't believe I was seeing these works with my own two eyes. The pictures from my glimpse into Jeong-min's life were now reality.

'Yeon-hwa, want to take a selfie together?' Sa-wol proposed.

'All right. Where should we take it?'

'How about in front of these plaster torsos?'

The torsos had been installed in the middle of the gallery space, facing each other – just the way Jeong-min had pictured in her final moments. But only one of them had a locket around its neck.

I pulled out the locket Jeong-min's ghost had left behind. It was identical. I wished I wouldn't have to trade it in to Hongseoksa Temple for my payment, because I was sure Su-min would appreciate it more.

Someone appeared behind us.

'This work defined me as an artist.'

It was Kim Su-min, the star of the exhibition. The recipient of our delivery. She looked slightly more mature than the woman I'd seen in Jeong-min's memories. More refined and relaxed, like she wasn't so desperate anymore to make a living and promote her art.

'Are you Ms Kim Su-min?'

'Yes. Would you like to know more about this work?'

'Absolutely,' I replied, tucking away Jeong-min's locket.

Serenely, Su-min explained, 'These torsos are the reason I'm under the Gold Foundation's patronage. They connect completely different styles of art together. It was the most popular piece at my first exhibition, and the critics loved it too. That was four years ago, and now I'm running a solo exhibition . . . The truth is, my best friend is the one who came up with this idea. I wish she could have been here too.'

I frowned. Something wasn't right. 'Wait, *four* years ago?'

'Yes. She passed in November, four years ago.'

The monk at Hongseoksa Temple had said that the dead couldn't be reincarnated if they didn't move on in three years. *Then what about Jeong-min?*

Sa-wol whispered, 'It looks like her locket won't need to go to the temple.'

Jeong-min was now trapped in limbo, neither living nor dead and never able to move on. I felt empty. I wondered why I wanted to cry, when both Jeong-min and Su-min appeared so calm. Now I knew why Jeong-min hadn't been in a hurry. She *couldn't* be reborn. There was something she wanted more than a new life: she wanted to see her best friend succeed in this one. The bittersweet exhibition tipped far into the flavour of the green tea dango.

So I pulled out the locket.

Su-min gasped, and when I handed it to her, she opened the cover. The picture inside was identical to hers.

'She wanted me to deliver these to you,' I said, holding out the shopping bag with the green tea dango. Su-min looked into the bag, then up at me, like she couldn't believe her eyes – and they were filled with light and wistfulness.

'But . . . how?'

I wished I could tell her everything, but I knew that the truth would only hurt her. I wondered where Jeong-min was now. Was she drifting on the wind? Had she become the wind itself? I wondered how she'd endured all these years, and thought back to her voice exclaiming, 'Time is money!' Time had been so important to her, and only the things she held most dear could make her spend all that time lost in her past.

I couldn't say a word.

'Congratulations on your first solo exhibition,' Sa-wol said in my place.

The soul that had silently cheered on her best friend would wander the earth for all eternity. Her innocent spirit was finally free, and although she could never again be the friend who had been at Su-min's side, she would leave behind a mark of her eternal, enduring love.

I prayed for their happiness.

5

The Fourth Customer and the Strawberry Chapssal-tteok

''Scuse me, do you sell strawberry chapssal-tteok?'

A few days after the exhibition, I got my fourth otherworldly customer: a boy with a bright yellow baseball cap pressed backwards over his head. He wore a clean, new T-shirt and bright blue dungarees, and held a handheld game console in his hand – and he couldn't stop looking around, like he'd never been to a shop on his own before.

I was still feeling melancholy from the fate of my last customer, and when I noticed that the boy had no shadow, I tasted something bitter on the tip of my tongue.

'Hey there. You're out late,' I said, bending down slightly to meet the boy's gaze. 'Do you know what this place is?'

'Uh-huh.'

'Can you tell me how old you are?'

'I'm ten years old.'

How could someone so young end up like this, I wondered. He looked so well cared for, like his family was looking after him with love.

The boy didn't notice my mood, though. He looked back at the little screen and said offhandedly, 'I'll go someplace else if you don't have them.'

'No, no. I can make strawberry chapssal-tteok for you,' I said quickly. 'I'm just feeling a little sad right now.'

'Why? I can pay you, you know,' the boy replied innocently over the comical background music from his game. He stuffed his hand into his pocket and brought out more than enough bills for some chapssal-tteok – but that wasn't what made me sad. I pictured him taking his purchase and disappearing out the door for good. Was this what it felt like to release a baby animal into the wild?

Still, the point of the Hwawoldang was to help the dead pass on. It was my job to give him one last taste of happiness. I was glad that he at least had his console with him, so he could have some fun after his death.

'Why're you staring? My nuna did that all the time, y'know.'

'You had a big sister?'

'Yeah. I want to give her the strawberry chapssal-tteok.'

'Is she . . .'

'She's alive.'

Then why are you here by yourself? I wanted to ask, but I was more mature than that now. I couldn't risk hurting the boy's feelings. Instead, I offered, 'Want to play together? I'm pretty good at games myself.'

'Really? Can you beat this boss for me?'

'I bet I could! I sell treats to ghosts, how hard could beating a fake monster be?'

'Okay! Then sit down over here. We can play in two-player mode,' the boy exclaimed, and held up the console. He clearly loved people. And that only made me feel worse. I brought a stool over and sat next to him.

The boy cheered as sound effects from the game filled the Hwawoldang. I decided to ask, 'What's your name?'

'I'm Park Ji-hwan! Hey, don't forget to grab that item.'

'Sorry, I'll be right there. And why did you order the chapssal-tteok?'

'I didn't order chapssal-tteok. I ordered *strawberry* chapssal-tteok.'

'Sorry again. But it's pretty much the same thing.'

'Nuh-uh. Nuna says they're totally different!'

'Were you good friends with your sister?'

'Um . . . I guess I should show you, huh?'

I awkwardly held out my hand. Ji-hwan took it and wrapped it tightly around the little console, which now connected our hands together.

'But,' he said, 'you have to promise to do something for me.'

I nodded.

'Okay, close your eyes,' he instructed.

I let my eyelids shut out the world, and soon a strange sensation came up my hand from the console, then my arm, and across my entire body. My consciousness was floating, flying off into the distance like a dream.

The sounds from the game went on.

❦

Ten-year-old Ji-hwan never felt comfortable around seventeen-year-old Yeon-ju.

When his dad had told him he was remarrying and Ji-hwan would get a big stepsister, he'd skipped around the living room with a big grin on his face. But the girl in the high school uniform didn't *feel* like a sister. More like another adult, like his new stepmum.

'Hi there. Nice to meet you, Ji-hwan.'

'Hi.'

'You can relax around me, okay?'

'Um . . . okay.'

Yeon-ju tried to break the ice. She talked to Ji-hwan and played fun pranks. But Ji-hwan just couldn't bring himself to feel differently.

Because Yeon-ju was preparing for university entrance exams, she was away at school and cram school every weekday until midnight. They almost never saw each other. They'd lived in the same house for a month, but still didn't feel like a family.

'You have to take initiative, Yeon-ju. Ji-hwan's too young; you can't expect him to try and make friends with you.'

'I know, Mum. But I'm busy with school.'

'Then could you try playing with him on weekends? He's been alone all this time. He doesn't show it, but Ji-hwan is a lonely boy.'

Yeon-ju couldn't count how many times her mum had told her to take care of Ji-hwan. But Yeon-ju was a teenager like any other. She did feel sorry for her new stepbrother, but he annoyed her, too. She didn't like having all this responsibility thrust on her shoulders. She wasn't old enough to be more independent, and he was too young for her to be real friends with. A brother closer to her age could be fun to tease, but doing that to a ten-year-old was too much like bullying.

Still, Yeon-ju worked up her courage. On weekend mornings, she'd go to Ji-hwan's room to say hello. But he would jump out of bed in a panic, sitting up straight with his hands clenched tightly on his lap, like he was talking to a teacher. So Yeon-ju would sit next to him and wonder how she could be his friend.

'What do you do with your friends at school?' she asked.

'We play *Brawl Stars*.'

'What's that?'

'Um, it's a game, and there's these monsters, and, um . . .'

He was sure she wouldn't understand, even if he explained as well as he could. She was sure it would be boring. An awkward silence fell over the room. It was hard for a ten-year-old and a seventeen-year-old to force themselves into a conversation when they barely knew each other.

Ji-hwan was supposed to call her 'Nuna', because Yeon-ju was now his older sister. But the girl – more like *adult* – next to him was so tall, and he was too intimidated to be curious. He didn't have any questions for her. But something told him that she might hate him if he didn't say anything.

So he took one terrifying step forward.

'Hey, Nuna, do you get good grades?'

He couldn't have chosen a worse question.

'Oh. No, not really.'

'What's your rank?'

'. . . Eighty-sixth in school.'

'Oh. Wow!'

There was another awkward silence. Yeon-ju knew Ji-hwan didn't mean to hurt her feelings, but it still stung to get questions like this. 'Ji-hwan, how about you?'

'I'm really good at maths.'

'How do you do on your tests?'

'Um . . . I got twelve out of thirty last time.'

'Can you really call that good?'

'Oh.'

Ji-hwan stuck out his lips. He'd got twelve whole

questions right – that was all ten fingers, and then two more – and he wished that had been enough to impress his new sister.

Yeon-ju read his disappointment like a book. 'Uh . . . I . . . um . . . hey, I really like that baseball cap!' she said, pointing at the hat hanging from the wardrobe. 'It's so . . . yellow!'

She nearly buried her face in her hands out of shame. Then three more minutes passed in silence, and she couldn't take it anymore – she said a stiff goodbye and rushed back to her room.

Ji-hwan was relieved, but he couldn't help the ache in his chest. What if his new sister hated him after all?

They weren't related by blood, but Ji-hwan and Yeon-ju were peas in a pod when it came to being passive introverts. The same thing happened every Saturday and Sunday, and soon they realized they were less awkward when their parents were around. They gave the stepsiblings pocket money to go buy ice cream at the local supermarket together, hoping they'd learn to get along better. But as soon as they'd paid the cashier and stepped out of the building, they were walking five paces apart.

What kind of jokes do I even tell a ten-year-old? Yeon-ju wondered.

I bet she'll think anything I do is immature, Ji-hwan thought.

They didn't hate each other, but they were so quiet and considerate that they didn't dare risk annoying each other. Nothing could seem to bridge their awkward gap.

❀

Ji-hwan spent his weekday afternoons playing tag at the playground with his friends Ji-tae and Na-ri. Soon they'd run so much they were all panting. But Ji-hwan was sure he could keep going. He could play tag for three more hours and never get tired. Na-ri, though, wiped the sweat from her brow and opened up the bag she'd left on the ground, pulling out a cold-water bottle with a handkerchief wrapped around it.

'I'm tired,' she said. 'I'm going to have some water and go home.'

'What? But it's not even dark yet.'

'My sister told me to come home early. She's making fried rice with eggs today.'

Ji-hwan grabbed her arm and begged her to stay for just two more rounds. But he'd held on too hard, and she lost her grip on the bottle. Cold water splashed all over her T-shirt.

Na-ri didn't get angry, though. 'She's buying me gummies for dessert, too,' she said maturely. She'd told Ji-hwan a few days ago that she got in trouble with her parents for eating too many snacks. But her sister, who started junior high this year, promised to buy her treats in secret. Na-ri was so excited to get more of her favourite snacks that she shook her wet T-shirt and got up without complaining, pushing her water bottle into her bag.

Two could still play tag, though. Ji-hwan grabbed Ji-tae's hand. 'Let's play a few more rounds!'

With his free hand, Ji-tae picked his nose. 'Okay, sounds good.'

'All right? Who's it?'

'Let's play rock-paper-scissors for it.'

They held up their hands, each ready to play –

'Ji-tae!'

A tall boy came over: Ji-tae's older brother. He was only in sixth grade, but to a ten-year-old, he looked as big and strong as a tiger. Ji-hwan's hand froze just before he could play rock.

'Let's go home, Ji-tae.'

'But we're playing tag.'

'Mum told me to pick you up on the way home.'

'Aw, man!'

'No complaining, Ji-tae. You're supposed to do what I say.'

Ji-tae deflated. He had to go home now. Ji-hwan had wanted to ask the older brother to join them for tag, too, but he looked so mature that he was too scared to say anything. Ji-tae's brother dusted dirt off Ji-tae's clothes and took his hand as they walked away together.

Ji-hwan couldn't believe it. He still had so much energy. He was sure he could play for hours still. But he didn't have anyone to play with. All he could do was kick around at the dirt under his feet.

Everyone had gone home with someone else. Ji-hwan thought about the meaning of the word 'alone'.

Wait . . . she doesn't have school today.

Yeon-ju's high school was closed to commemorate the school's anniversary. She was supposed to be at home. Ji-hwan imagined his sister coming to the playground to pick him up.

That only made him want to go home. His stepsister never bought him snacks in secret or came to get him from the playground, but having a quiet sister around was better than being alone.

Meanwhile, Yeon-ju lay on the sofa, enjoying her

day off. Mock exams loomed menacingly over her, but she tried not to think about those. Today, she raided the fridge and ate all the snacks she wanted. A weekday at home was a student's humble paradise.

She brought out her handheld game console. She was playing the most popular game at school, with different stages that had a big boss battle at the end. She'd been stuck on one boss for days, but this time, she was ready. She lay on her stomach on the sofa, her chin resting on a cushion. She had the entire afternoon to focus –

'I'm home.'

The door opened, and Ji-hwan entered.

'You're early,' Yeon-ju said. She didn't get up.

'It's because my friends went home early today.'

'Okay. Remember to wash your hands and feet,' Yeon-ju said, only half-listening, and looked back at her screen. But for some reason, she couldn't concentrate anymore. She'd seen Ji-hwan's face when he came inside. He'd looked so sad. *What do ten-year-olds have to be sad about?* she wondered, and peered into the bathroom as Ji-hwan washed his feet. 'Did something happen?' she asked.

'No.'

Ji-hwan wanted to be honest. He wanted to tell

her everything he'd felt. But he didn't want his stepsister to hate him.

But Ji-hwan was a terrible liar, especially because he was only ten. Yeon-ju asked in disbelief, 'Then why're you home so early?'

'Because I was alone.'

This time, Yeon-ju heard him. She hadn't expected that answer. She could already picture poor Ji-hwan, standing awkwardly by himself in the playground. And suddenly, she felt like she'd left the poor ten-year-old on his own when she could have been there for him.

Ji-hwan, though, couldn't read so much into his older stepsister. He was sure he'd fooled her, since he hadn't *said* exactly how he felt. He was alone in the playground. That was just fact. He had no idea that his naïveté only moved his sister more.

Yeon-ju couldn't sit by any longer. 'Do you want to play this game with me?' she offered, holding out her console as Ji-hwan stood with his feet still wet.

Ji-hwan brightened instantly. Game consoles were supposed to be for *teenagers*, and his new sister was letting him try one.

'It's a game where you fight monsters. I guess it might be a bit hard.'

'No! I want to play! Please?'

'Okay, let me show you how it works.'

Yeon-ju sat Ji-hwan next to her on the sofa and let him take the controls. She wanted to play for herself, too, but cheering up her downcast brother felt more fulfilling. Yeon-ju *wanted* to stop being awkward, because they were supposed to be a family. She was sure this would make her feel better about not having developed a closer bond with him yet.

'You move the characters with these buttons. And you can attack when you press this button.'

'Okay. Let me try that.'

'Did you eat dinner?'

'No.'

'Want to eat something while you play?'

'No, I don't have to,' Ji-hwan replied. He was clearly too focused on the game.

Must be nice, being ten. Life is so simple, Yeon-ju thought, and went to the fridge. She pulled out a container of cut strawberries, apples and oranges her mum had prepared. Ji-hwan barely paid any attention to the fruit, but he did make sure to pop a few strawberries into his mouth.

'You like strawberries?' Yeon-ju asked.

'Yeah.'

'I like strawberries too.'

'That's cool.'

'Come on, I bet you didn't even hear what I said,' Yeon-ju replied with a chuckle.

Ji-hwan was so absorbed that he looked like his survival depended on beating the monsters, *right now*. Yeon-ju was proud of herself for lending him her console. She wasn't getting any extra pocket money for being a good babysitter, but watching him have so much fun made her happy.

Soon, they'd finished all the fruit. But Yeon-ju still wanted a snack.

'I'm going to pick up something for us to eat, okay?' she said, pulling on her coat.

'Okay.'

'You could at least say thank you.'

'When you come back.'

'Cheeky, aren't we?'

Yeon-ju's favourite local dessert shop sold a variety of handmade chapssal-tteok – and the strawberry flavour was out of this world. Each piece of white chapssal-tteok was filled with red bean paste and half a fresh strawberry, and overall resembled a hamster curled into a ball. Yeon-ju could never resist the adorable shape, and got two to take home.

Ji-hwan was still lost in the game when Yeon-ju returned. 'I got us some strawberry chapssal-tteok. Want some?'

'Oh. I don't like chapssal-tteok.'

'This is *strawberry* chapssal-tteok. There's a big difference.'

Ji-hwan put down the console and looked closely at the chapssal-tteok. And when Yeon-ju unwrapped the plastic packaging and held one out to him, he received it, and took a bite at the same time as she bit into hers. He tasted the natural sweetness of the red bean, and the sweet-and-sour flavour of the strawberry, all wrapped in the sticky chewiness of the glutinous rice.

'Chapssal-tteok usually makes you thirsty, but the strawberry is so moist you don't feel it,' Yeon-ju explained as she chewed.

'It's so good!' Ji-hwan cried, his mouth still full. He quickly took another excited bite, because he couldn't get enough of the chewy texture. Even after the chapssal-tteok was gone, he kept chewing at nothing.

Finally, Yeon-ju looked him in the eye. 'Now do you have something to say to me?'

'Thank you,' Ji-hwan said with a full ninety-degree bow.

Yeon-ju couldn't help smiling at his formality. She ruffled his hair, getting rice powder on his head. He looked like he'd been snowed on. Ji-hwan saw her giggle, and finally felt like she wasn't so intimidating after all.

Ji-hwan wasn't too young to learn the simple lesson that happiness was multiplied when you shared it with someone else.

❀

Before they knew it, Ji-hwan and Yeon-ju were friends. Yeon-ju would let him play her game, asking him to beat the bosses for her. And Ji-hwan, although he pretended he didn't want to, played as much as he wanted. Soon, he was glued to the console even as the sun set after dinner and the world went dark.

'Time for bed, Ji-hwan.'

'Aw, Mum. Can I fight just one more boss?'

'Honey, it's already nine. And did Yeon-ju give you permission to play?'

'Yeah.'

Their mum gave Yeon-ju a glance to ask if she'd let him use her console. She smiled back and nodded.

'See?' Ji-hwan said.

He loved his big sister now. She always let him

play her game, and she took his side, too. He wasn't just playing for himself, either. He stayed up late every night, rubbing his sleepy eyes, because he wanted to thank Yeon-ju by beating the monsters she couldn't beat for herself.

Ji-hwan even stopped asking Na-ri and Ji-tae to stay later in the playground after school. 'Are you going home already?' Ji-tae asked when Ji-hwan picked up his bag before anyone else.

'Yeah. I'm playing a game on a *console*.'

'No way! Did your mum buy it for you?'

'It's my nuna's.'

'I didn't know you had a sister!'

'Yeah! She's in high school, and she's really tall.'

Ji-hwan would never be alone in the playground again. Now he was the first one to wave his friends goodbye. He felt so proud when he told them that *his* sister was in high school, which almost made her a grown-up. Each day, he would skip home from the playground, looking forward to the big smile on her face when he beat the next boss, looking forward to being her friend. He was never lonely, even when he was walking alone. His sister was his friend, and slowly, he was learning to be mature.

STRAWBERRY CHAPSSAL-TTEOK: 1,500 WON

On the way back, Ji-hwan spotted Yeon-ju's usual dessert shop. The strawberry chapssal-tteok from last time seemed to whisper his name from just behind the glass, and in the blink of an eye, he was walking inside. They looked so soft and delicious, and he could already taste the sweet and sticky feeling in his mouth. But the strawberry chapssal-tteok was more than that. Strawberry chapssal-tteok meant sitting close to Yeon-ju and learning to play her game.

''Scuse me, can I have some strawberry chapssal-tteok?' he asked.

The manager smiled. 'Of course, dear. How many would you like?'

'Um . . .'

In his head, Ji-hwan did the maths. He had one 5,000-won bill, and he wanted to make sure the whole family got one each. But four strawberry chapssal-tteok would cost 6,000 won. He just didn't have enough. And he wasn't crafty or friendly enough to ask the manager for a discount.

'Three, please,' he finally said, looking down at his bill.

'For sharing with your parents? How sweet of you.'

'Oh. Um, yeah.'

'Here you are. I'm sure they're so proud of you, young man.'

'Thank you,' Ji-hwan replied.

He couldn't stop glancing into the bag, not even as he got to their condo, stepped into the lift, and unlocked the door. As soon as he was in the kitchen, he took out the three strawberry chapssal-tteok and laid them out in a row. The rice powder made them look almost like fuzzy lumps of fur, but he knew that inside were fresh strawberry halves nestled in red bean paste. His mouth watered as he remembered the flavour. He gulped and put a finger on one of the strawberry chapssal-tteok. It was so round and soft, and he wanted to eat it so badly. But he stopped.

Ji-hwan had 500 won left in his pocket. He went to the calendar and tried to count the days until he got more pocket money – and realized that tomorrow was circled. They were going on their first family outing since their parents had got married. He knew he wouldn't remember the strawberry chapssal-tteok while he was playing in the mountain creek with the family. So he decided to get a permanent marker and write on the plastic packaging of the strawberry chapssal-tteok.

Then he threw himself onto the sofa, lying on his stomach again and staring into the screen. Now all he could think about was his sister. He kept on playing, beating monster after monster, but the newest boss just wouldn't go down.

'Come on . . . I have to beat this one for Nuna,' he whispered, and slowly dozed off as the sun set outside. He barely thought about resisting before he was completely limp, blanketed by the light of dusk as he slept.

The plastic packaging of the strawberry chapssal-tteok shone in the light like early evening stars, each labelled 'Mum', 'Dad' and 'Nuna'.

❀

Yeon-ju was busy the next morning picking out an outfit for their family trip. They were going to take so many pictures together, and she wanted to look great. Unfortunately, she'd slept in, and didn't have much time.

Meanwhile, Ji-hwan was still asleep. His mum tried to shake him awake, but he'd gone into such a deep sleep yesterday that he still wanted more rest.

'Ugh, come on!' Yeon-ju finally complained, pulling off his blanket and sitting him up. It was already noon by the time Ji-hwan woke up in his pyjamas and said a half-dazed 'good morning' to his sister.

Yeon-ju was impatient to leave. She quickly got Ji-hwan's outfit ready for him, but even as she complained, she made sure to grab his bright yellow baseball cap.

'Nuna, can I play the game today?'

'Ji-hwan, we're late because *you* slept in. No gaming,' Yeon-ju said. She couldn't believe that was the first thing on his mind, when she was desperate to get going soon.

'Please?'

Unfortunately, their mum had had enough. When she found Ji-hwan asleep on the sofa with the console last night, she'd taken it away and warned Yeon-ju not to lend it to Ji-hwan again. She didn't want him to keep staying up late.

'Ji-hwan,' Yeon-ju said, 'you can't play anymore.'

Ji-hwan's eyes flew open. 'Why?'

'Because all you do is play, play, play, and then sleep in the next morning.'

'But I need to beat one more boss.'

'Forget it. You're not going to beat that one, ever.'

'Come on, just one more time! Please?'

'No,' Yeon-ju said firmly. Her mum had drawn the line, and she couldn't argue.

As for Ji-hwan, for the first time, Yeon-ju scared him more than his parents. He wasn't brave enough to argue, but something didn't feel right. *But I'm doing this for her. Why is Nuna getting angry at me?*

Ji-hwan only wanted to play because Yeon-ju had asked him to beat the boss monsters for her. He couldn't believe she was scolding him for doing something she wanted him to do. He hated her, and thought she was being unfair, because siblings weren't supposed to get you in trouble. That was what parents did. She was only a teenager. She wasn't supposed to be a real adult. *I even bought the strawberry chapssal-tteok for her.* He pouted even more when he remembered the treats he'd got for everyone but himself. Ji-hwan wished he'd eaten her portion, and almost said so.

Meanwhile, Yeon-ju was frustrated because Ji-hwan acted like he hadn't done anything wrong. *He* was the one who'd slept in, and *he* was the one who'd got in trouble for playing games all day. 'Hey, don't give me that look,' she said sternly, hands on her hips. 'It's not my fault you're in trouble.'

Ji-hwan glared. 'But why am I in trouble?'

'Because today's an important day, and you *slept in*!'

'But why can't I play the game?'

'The game is *mine*, Ji-hwan. I let you borrow it. It's not yours, and I can do whatever I want with it.'

'That's not fair.'

'And you're being naughty!'

Ji-hwan felt like he'd been punched. His mind went blank, and he couldn't believe he'd been happy to be friends with Yeon-ju. He felt pathetic.

Yeon-ju didn't understand, though, and stomped away. Soon, their mum came in to make sure Ji-hwan was dressed, and the family drove away in pointed silence.

❀

Yeon-ju was disappointed that Ji-hwan hadn't got up in time. Ji-hwan was disappointed that Yeon-ju had scolded him. Their parents glanced back through the mirror worriedly.

'Kids, you're in big trouble with your mother if you don't make up by the time we get there,' their dad said with a smile, taking a sip of water.

'He started it!'

'She said I was naughty!'

Ji-hwan and Yeon-ju glared, fists clenched and arms crossed respectively. They knew deep down that both were at fault, but it was hard to admit they were wrong. Ten and seventeen was a large difference, but both were still too young to graciously own up to their mistakes.

As their old car sped on, Yeon-ju took a deep breath and turned. 'Ji-hwan,' she said.

But Ji-hwan was still angry. He made a point of shifting further away, pressing himself close to the door.

'Ugh, can you stop?' Yeon-ju complained, now even more irritated. She gave him one last look and didn't say another word.

Half an hour later, the car was on the highway. The sky slowly grew dark with clouds, and while their parents checked the weather at their destination, droplets of rain spattered against the windows. The wipers quickly got to work. Yeon-ju, meanwhile, stared out at the drab grey clouds and pushed her hands deeper into the pockets of her windbreaker. Her fingers brushed against the packaged strawberry chapssal-tteok Ji-hwan had left on the table.

She shut her eyes and thought of the day they first met.

❦

Yeon-ju was never good at talking to boys.

Her parents divorced for what they called 'irreconcilable differences in character'. Then she was alone with her mum until high school. She didn't care for boys – the only boys in her life were actors and idols anyway – and she'd been hooked to a reality show about spoiled children and their reign of terror over their families.

Why do people even raise boys? They're all monsters!

She'd seen so many parents reduced to sobs by rebellious sons that eventually the kids in the playground looked more like selfish little monkeys than cute children.

Then, her mother announced she'd be remarrying – and Yeon-ju would have a younger stepbrother.

'No!' Yeon-ju had shrieked. 'He's going to mess up this whole house!'

'Please, Yeon-ju. Try to understand. He's seven years younger than you – try to give him a chance.'

'No way. If he misbehaves, he's getting the boot!'

'Honey, please.'

There was no way Yeon-ju could stop the wedding, and fortunately, her stepdad seemed like a good man. What else could she do? Yeon-ju told herself that she would live with her new little brother – and if he decided to misbehave like the other boys she saw on TV, she would make sure he regretted it.

She was still seething when she met Ji-hwan.

'Hi,' she said sullenly.

'Hello, Nuna.'

Ji-hwan was nothing like the kids she'd seen on her reality shows. He clasped his hands politely over his belly button and bowed so deep she felt uncomfortable. Ji-hwan seemed to be scared of her, especially because she was taller and had bigger hands and feet than most of her friends. Now Yeon-ju didn't know what to do. She'd been so busy planning to punish her stepbrother that she'd never thought about being *nice* to such a shy, quiet boy. He stiffened like a scared little dog whenever he had to sit near her.

'Nuna, what school do you go to?'

'Semyeong Girls' High School.'

'Wow . . . you're in *high school*.'

'There's nothing "wow" about that . . . is there?'
'Um . . . yeah.'

Ji-hwan was wary of Yeon-ju, but always wanted to be closer to her. And no matter how much he tried to hide it, Yeon-ju could tell in an instant. Before the wedding, they'd all gone out for dinner together, and Ji-hwan had politely placed the napkins and cutlery in front of her. Those little gestures showed Yeon-ju that her new little brother only ever wanted to please her.

I was wrong, she thought. *The stuff I see on TV isn't always real.*

And so, she changed her attitude. She opened her heart. She decided to be a good big sister to Ji-hwan. Yeon-ju's friends argued with their siblings, but they always made up and took each other's sides in the end. She wanted to know what that was like.

But things didn't get off to a great start. Making friends with Ji-hwan wasn't as easy as she hoped. She just couldn't take the initiative to be a friendly big sister.

❀

Those memories ran through Yeon-ju's mind before the family left the house that day. She'd stopped for a drink of water when she spotted three packaged strawberry chapssal-tteok, with one labelled 'Nuna'. Destiny was being mean that day, showing her Ji-hwan's gift right after she'd lost her temper with him.

Ugh, why didn't I see this earlier?

Still, that didn't make her feel completely better. Ji-hwan *had* been a bit of a brat, even if he could be considerate sometimes.

Yeon-ju opened her eyes in the car. Ji-hwan had fallen asleep next to her, as if he hadn't slept in enough. His mouth was shut and his nostrils flared softly. His yellow cap was pressed backwards over his head, and his cheeks looked softer than a pair of chapssal-tteok dumplings.

Maybe I should have just let him keep playing.

It wasn't long before she felt sleepy, too. Yeon-ju shifted in her seat, crossing her arms as the car sped on. Her parents were talking about something, but it was all white noise to her ears, and she could only make out snippets of the conversation –

'. . . a lot of rain.'

'How many umbrellas . . . trunk . . . ?'

'. . . three.'

She heard thumping all around her, growing louder and louder by the second, but she didn't feel like wondering if it was the rain. She was so comfortable now, like she was about to drift off into her dreams –

'. . . truck's acting a bit strange . . .'

'. . . I'll get ahead . . .'

Prophecy didn't always take the form of words. Sometimes, people spotted certain things that simply gave them a feeling – a feeling that could change the course of the future. What did Yeon-ju happen to see earlier that very day?

Ji-hwan's seatbelt.

She'd *wanted* to remind him to buckle up, but he'd been such a brat that morning that she'd decided to say nothing. If only she'd made sure he was buckled in – if only she'd spoken up –

'That container's *shaking*.'

'What's happening?'

The dozing truck driver made a tragic error, sending his vehicle slipping on the rainy highway. The container it towed soon hung precariously over the family car, then tipped – and before anyone could think of slamming the brakes, the car spun violently until its bumper hit the guardrail. Then came another impact, and then another, as the cars behind them slammed into the growing pile-up and sent the poor Sonata sliding into the distance.

A plume of grey smoke mingled with the clouds overhead.

Yeon-ju couldn't tell if she was awake or asleep. All she knew was that blood was running down her cheeks. But she still reached out, her hand grasping her little brother's shoulder. He sat with his head bowed, completely still. And she was overwhelmed by regret.

Why didn't I buckle him in?

❀

Then I was in the Hwawoldang again, and I slowly took my hand off Ji-hwan's handheld console. He still looked so playful. His regrets had been taken away when he died, and only the living could mourn for his terrible fate.

'Did you order the strawberry chapssal-tteok to see your sister again?' I asked, bending low again to meet his gaze.

Ji-hwan's eyes were dark, but sparkled with honesty. 'Um, it's not really that. But she probably didn't get to eat the chapssal-tteok I bought for her.'

'I'm sorry. You must be so sad.'

'Nope. I'm going to have an even better life next time.'

'Really? Tell me.'

'Next time, I'm gonna be the world's best pro gamer!' he cried, giving me a thumbs-up. I had to admire him for being so optimistic, even in death. 'And I'm going to be like my nuna.'

'A pro gamer who's just like your sister, huh?'

'Yeah. And if I have a little sibling, I'm going to be the best big brother, too!'

Without thinking, I pulled the yellow cap from Ji-hwan's head. Blood had crusted on his scalp – the first time I'd seen signs of death on a spirit. I took a wet wipe to gently clean it off, and placed the cap back on his head.

'I bet Nuna hates me now,' he said. 'Because the last thing I did was annoy her.'

I couldn't let that slide. 'That's not true.'

He looked up, eyes shining.

Meeting his gaze, I went on: 'How could she hate her own family?'

I thought of Grandma. We'd never been as close as Ji-hwan and Yeon-ju, but I didn't resent Grandma anymore. I had so much time to think about her while I worked at the Hwawoldang. I wondered if things might have been different between us if I'd been more affectionate and open.

It was time to make Ji-hwan his strawberry chapssal-tteok. And fortunately, it was just the right season. I washed each strawberry thoroughly under running water to preserve the soft sweetness, and cut off the stems. Then I dried each strawberry to make sure the red bean paste I kept in the fridge would cling properly. Once each strawberry was perfectly coated, I rolled them into spheres. The chapssal-tteok was made with a 1:1 mixture of glutinous rice powder and water, plus a tablespoon of sugar. Once it was all mixed up and heated, it formed a watery white dough that I could wrap around each ball of paste-coated strawberry.

Before I knew it, Ji-hwan was hopping in place. The shop floor seemed to creak each time he landed.

'D'you think Nuna liked me too?'

'Did you like your sister, Ji-hwan?'

'Yeah! I always wanted to have a big sister. I wanted to tell my friends that my sister was in *high school*, and she even let me play her games. I wanted to go to the playground with her, and eat strawberries together. There are so many things I wanted to do with her!'

'Then I'm sure she loved you very much, Ji-hwan,' I said confidently.

Ji-hwan didn't seem convinced. 'She never said that.'

'Words aren't the only way to express love, you know,' I explained.

'Oh. Then how do you tell someone you love them?'

You had to cake together an assortment of ingredients to make a proper tteok. It reminded me of Ji-hwan and Yeon-ju, a pair of awkward new stepsiblings who'd wanted to become one family. And although destiny had torn them apart, their determination hadn't died. I made sure that the strawberry and the red bean paste were properly bundled together in the dough.

I couldn't answer Ji-hwan's last question, but my fingers were busy rolling the chapssal-tteok in rice powder. It would make sure the chapssal-tteok didn't stick to everything it touched, and gave it a dusty texture.

'There we are!'

Ji-hwan danced for joy, his backside waggling like an excited puppy's. I held out one chapssal-tteok towards him before I wrapped up the remaining four.

'Wait,' Ji-hwan said, pulling out a pen and paper

from the front pocket of his dungarees. 'Can I write a letter?'

'For your sister?'

'Uh-huh. Can you give this to her, too? My nuna has a mole on her right cheek.'

Yet again, I knew I couldn't refuse the delivery request. 'All right,' I said, 'but you have to tell me the name of her school.'

Ji-hwan gobbled up his chapssal-tteok on the spot, then got to work on his letter with his cheeks still puffy. It made him look warm and cozy somehow, like he'd been wrapped up in warm dough, too.

I expected Ji-hwan to leave his handheld console on the countertop. But the yellow cap was there instead. Ji-hwan grinned when he saw my response, and something told me he'd be born a mischievous boy in his next life. I opened the door for him, and he bounded outside without looking back.

'Huh?'

When I finally spotted his handheld console on one of the folding chairs, I grabbed it and rushed back outside.

But Ji-hwan was gone, and the console scattered to dust in my hand.

The night seemed utterly empty, except for the sparkling light of the moon.

❀

Early the next morning, I told Sa-wol what had happened and arranged to meet in front of the Hwa-woldang. Yeon-ju's school wasn't far, so we could reach her on her way to classes.

There was just one problem:

'What on *earth* is that outfit, Sa-wol? You're going to scare her off!'

Sa-wol's usual hanbok was eye-catching enough. But today, he was in full shaman costume – bright primary colours, dizzying patterns, flowing robes and all. This was not going to help our case.

'You'll have to live with it,' he said with a shrug. 'My powers wane in the morning, and I need these clothes to make up for it.'

'You're going to perform an entire gut ritual on the *street*?'

'No, no.'

'She'll think you're creepy,' I insisted.

'Don't worry, Yeon-hwa,' he replied easily. His prayer beads sparkled even more in the morning sun. 'The letter will draw the sister to me, like destiny.'

I sighed. I was sure I'd have to calm poor Yeon-ju down.

'Let's see now,' Sa-wol said as we made our way to the high school. 'It should be around here somewhere . . . Whoa!'

Without warning, he tripped over his shoelaces. Ji-hwan's letter fluttered out of his grasp.

Several trucks passed by on the street next to us, sending the letter flying in a gust of wind. It landed on the foot of a girl in a school uniform.

She was tall, with a mole on her right cheek.

Yeon-ju.

A warm, gentle breeze blew past, and the hairs on my arms stood on end as I realized what was happening. Sa-wol was already trotting up to the girl, his sleeves flapping behind him. Yeon-ju backed away in shock, which wasn't a surprise to anyone, but Sa-wol held out a friendly hand and smiled.

'Excuse me, miss. I dropped that letter, but I don't need it back. It's yours.'

'What? No, this isn't mine.'

'We're here on delivery from a traditional sweetshop called the Hwawoldang – yes, Yeon-hwa, I said *we*!'

I jammed myself between Sa-wol and the poor

teenager. I had to make sure this got done right. 'You're Park Yeon-ju, right? Someone ordered some strawberry chapssal-tteok for you.'

'Who?'

'It's all in this letter,' I said, pointing.

Yeon-ju looked curiously at the letter as she unfolded it. In that moment, it felt like we'd been transported to another world – the morning sun seemed to shine brighter for an instant as it perched on her head, the streets were silent, and no cars or passersby would interrupt us now.

Slowly, Yeon-ju's eyes moved down the page.

HOW TO BEAT THE FINAL BOSS

Dear Nuna, if you want to beat the final boss, go to the secret forest before the boss battle and get the golden key. I kept trying after I died, and now I know how to win. So now you should win and be happy. Sorry I was late. Sorry I slept in. Please don't hate me. I was happy to get a sister. I wasn't sad when my friends went home without me. Please remember me sometimes and be happy with Mum and Dad. I'll miss you. A lot. But I'll be okay. So please live for a long, long time.

The next gust of wind roared past like a dragon, snatching the letter from Yeon-ju's hand. It seemed to flap its wings as it disappeared into the sky, and no matter how much Sa-wol tried to grab it, the letter departed with all the inevitability of Ji-hwan's fate.

Then Yeon-ju brought her hands to her ears, like she was straining to catch a voice. But she couldn't say a word, and when I saw her eyes grow red, I pulled out a handkerchief and placed it in her hand.

'He was thinking of you to the end,' I told her. 'We can see the dead, Yeon-ju. He passed on thinking of you.'

'Oh . . .' Yeon-ju whispered, her hands trembling.

Destiny had brought his voice to her, and she knew we were telling the truth.

'I . . . I should have buckled him in,' she said, and burst into sobs. I pulled her into a hug as she wept like a lost child. 'It was all my fault . . . all my fault . . .'

I said reassuringly, 'Don't blame yourself. Ji-hwan never did. He wanted you to be happy.'

'. . . But . . . I . . .'

Sunlight filled Sa-wol's prayer beads as he placed an encouraging hand on her shoulder. 'He's gone somewhere even better than his game world,' he said.

Then she was wailing, held tight in the arms of two strangers. Each tear was filled with guilt, sorrow and an indelible wistfulness. Her emotions were piled together like the layers of a well-baked pastry, but the only word I had for those complicated feelings was 'love'. That was what she'd wanted to express to her new little brother; and now she would never get that chance.

The dead had granted their forgiveness, and the living were left to long for the lost. What more could anyone do, but move past the regrets?

6

Sa-wol's Story, and the Chestnut Yanggaeng of Goodbye

The Hwawoldang was open, but I was alone.

Not a single spirit came through the door. No one wanted to say goodbye to this world tonight, I guessed. All I could do was stand behind the counter with my chin on my hand, staring out at the darkened sky.

I wished boredom could be fun. It was so quiet that even cleaning sounded interesting. But as I grabbed the feather duster, I spotted the calendar and realized just how long I'd been running the Hwawoldang – not from the date on the calendar, but by the layer of dust on the paper.

Am I doing a good job?

I still had so many questions about the Hwawoldang. I had to admit, it was interesting helping the dead pass on. But did I really *love* this work? I wasn't sure. I didn't quite *feel* like I was the owner of this place, because there was so much I still didn't know. It was always like this. Growing up, I'd ask about my parents, but Grandma wouldn't tell me much – and I never tried to pry. Why not? Why did I simply let things lie?

The feather duster brushed furiously over the surfaces, sending dust motes flying under the lights.

'Meow.'

The black cat was a regular at the Hwawoldang now, and I wasn't too surprised when, for the first time, she brought me a folded-up note.

'Is this from a customer?' I asked her.

'Meeeeow.'

I opened the note. It was an order.

1 serving of the Hwawoldang's specialty red chestnut yanggaeng, to be picked up in three days.

The order was simple, but something about the paper smelled antique – not *old* or musty, but somehow *mysterious*. As for the cat? Her work was done and she buried her face in her bowl of kibble.

Red chestnut yanggaeng was one of the Hwawoldang's signature products. It was seasonal and made only in small batches. Grandma had stopped making them when she got sick.

I really loved those, I thought. Grandma would set some aside for me sometimes, and I loved the explosion of forest-scented flavour and the sweetness that you could only get in yanggaeng. I'd never been brave enough to ask for more of the jelly, though.

Thinking back, Mum and Dad loved that yanggaeng, too.

Is the recipe in here? I wondered, flipping through the booklet. I found green tea yanggaeng and chestnut yanggaeng, but nothing about *red* chestnut yanggaeng. You couldn't get that colour with a normal recipe, because the primary ingredient, red bean paste, was actually closer to black in colour – which swallowed up any hint of red you could add.

If I wanted to add bright, eye-catching colours to a batch of yanggaeng, I had to use *white* bean paste, which was what the green tea yanggaeng used. But the bottom of the recipe clearly stated: *Use RED bean paste for chestnut yanggaeng*.

Red beans and white beans weren't two different colours of the same bean. Each had a subtly distinct flavour, and chestnut yanggaeng tasted much better with red bean paste. The customer clearly ordered the Hwawoldang's specialty red chestnut yanggaeng, too, which meant I had to use red bean paste and somehow bring out the colour red in the jelly. Only Grandma, who invented the recipe, could pull off something like that.

But she didn't leave me the recipe.

I cradled my head in my hands. I wished someone could be here to answer all my questions. I picked up my phone and scrolled down to Sa-wol's contact information. Something told me he wasn't asleep yet. I didn't have anyone else to turn to, but suddenly, I felt shy about asking for his help.

'Meow!'

The cat leapt up without warning and bumped into my finger.

Before I knew it, the call was going through.

Even if I hung up now, he'd know I'd called his number. What was I supposed to say? *Your Honor, my cat made me do it. No, really! It was her fault!*

'Hello?'

I didn't even have time to fumble and drop my phone. I couldn't make excuses now. I had to sound natural. He'd think I was weird if I called out of the blue in the middle of the night and hung up without a word!

'Yeon-hwa, it's *midnight*.'

'Um . . . I'm at the Hwawoldang right now.'

'Yes, and?'

Something about Sa-wol had been bothering me for a while. He was hiding something, not least the secret that was going to save me from financial disaster. That was frustrating, yes, but it only made me want to learn more about him. This wasn't like me at all.

'The *cat* pressed the call button,' I said.

'. . . Are you talking in your sleep?'

I could practically *see* the disbelief on his smirking face. I cleared my throat, fingers running over the yanggaeng page of the recipe booklet as I collected myself. 'I got a preorder from a spirit,' I explained. 'It's supposed to be ready in three days, but I can't figure out the recipe. I thought you might know something about it.'

'What's the order?'

'The Hwawoldang's specialty red chestnut yanggaeng. Do you know how to make red yanggaeng while using red bean paste?'

'Ah,' Sa-wol said with a hint of recognition. 'Your grandmother's secret recipe. That's going to be a tough one.'

I pulled out a pen and paper. 'I don't care how hard it is. Just give me the recipe!'

But Sa-wol said simply, 'I don't know it. I only know where to source the secret ingredient.'

'*Where?*'

The silence was filled only by the ticking of the clock and the distant soft footsteps of the black cat.

'Hongseoksa Temple,' Sa-wol finally said.

I dropped my pen and clutched at the phone. 'Who on earth gets yanggaeng ingredients from a *temple?*'

'Your grandmother.'

My steps took me from behind the counter to the front door, and soon I was staring down at the mailbox. At the overflowing bills that would have banged on the door if they had fists. The Hwa-woldang's owner was gone, but the shop still lived, still needed to be maintained and looked after. The yellow baseball cap still sat on the counter.

'All right, fine,' I replied. I had to pay off the bills, and I had to learn Grandma's secret recipe. I had all the reasons in the world to go to Hongseoksa Temple again.

'Then I'll come with you,' Sa-wol said without missing a beat. 'I have business there in three days.'

'Okay. I'll see you then,' I said, hanging up.

It sounded so simple, but why did I feel so uneasy

about going to the temple again? I felt like I'd been handed an assignment with no instructions, and couldn't shake that feeling even as I locked up and headed home in the dark. As soon as I was inside, I took a shower and went to bed.

For the first time since Grandma's death, I had a nightmare.

I heard a loud klaxon, and bloody shadows were suddenly wrapping around me, whispering into my ears. Dreams belonged not to the sleeper, but to the mysterious weaver of dreams. I was locked in a story told by another, and there was no escape.

When I finally opened my eyes, my back was clammy with sweat.

For the next three days, I practised making standard chestnut yanggaeng. And although nothing could beat Grandma's twist on the original, I had to admit I was doing a decent job. I decided to pack a couple of batches for Sa-wol and the monk at Hongseoksa Temple, fitting them into a small shopping bag alongside a bottle of water and a pack of tissues.

Sa-wol arrived not long afterwards – mercifully in ordinary street clothes this time, probably because he didn't need to use his powers – and I handed him his portion of the yanggaeng.

'What's this?' he asked.

'Chestnut yanggaeng. Try it with cold green tea.'

Sa-wol knitted his brow. 'You could have fooled me. What is this *shape*? This is one of your failures, isn't it?'

'I should have known better than to try and fool a shaman.'

'Ah, so I've been demoted from "supplier" to "waste disposal".'

'If you don't like it, I'll take it back,' I said with crossed arms.

'No, no,' Sa-wol said, not sounding unhappy in the least. 'I'm sure it'll taste better than it looks – and the funny shape is a plus, if you ask me.' I couldn't hate him for that, even if he could be a little immature sometimes.

It was a long walk to Hongseoksa Temple, but only a few minutes by car, and we'd met so late in the afternoon that I didn't want to risk being late. 'Let's take a taxi,' I suggested partway through the trip.

'I'd rather not,' Sa-wol said tersely.

'But it's so hot today. We can drop in and come back quickly by car.'

'No. We'll walk.'

Nothing could sway Sa-wol. He pretended not to hear my complaining, walking with his fingers interlocked on the back of his head as he chatted about learning to enjoy the afternoon sun.

'Looks like you really love hoofing it everywhere,' I pointed out. 'You said no to the taxi last time, too.'

'What's wrong with walking? I rather enjoy taking in the sights.'

I looked around. 'Yes, I love taking in the concrete jungle.'

'There's some grass up ahead.'

'Sa-wol, you're hiding something,' I accused gently, but he didn't respond.

We went on, passing one twisty road after another, but the temple still seemed so far away. I hadn't got much sleep the last few nights because of the nightmare, and soon I couldn't walk anymore.

'Sa-wol, can we *please* take a taxi?'

'It's not much further now, Yeon-hwa.'

'I'm not feeling so good. Please?'

With each step towards Hongseoksa Temple, I felt more and more like those creepy nightmare shadows were still hanging off my shoulders. I couldn't take it anymore. Who cared what Sa-wol thought? He couldn't say no to a free ride. I pulled out my phone and opened up the taxi app.

'Go ahead without me,' he said primly. 'I'll follow you on foot.'

My jaw dropped. '*Why?*'

'We don't *have* to go there together,' Sa-wol said with a shrug.

'What do you have against taxis?'

'What do you say to taking the bus instead?'

'There's no bus service here.'

'Then I'll see you at Hongseoksa Temple.'

The taxi I'd hailed spotted us. As it approached, I wondered what it was about taxis that bothered Sa-wol to the point that he refused to use them at all. With an irritated glare, I demanded, 'You need to tell me what's going on, Sa-wol. Why all the secrecy? Did Grandma put you up to all this?'

'No.'

I wished I could just let this go. He could have a perfectly good reason for not liking taxis. But I felt rejected somehow by the way Sa-wol refused to answer my questions. Did he not want to be in a car with me? Did he not like my company? But wasn't he the one who'd offered to come along? I couldn't stop asking questions – not out loud – and soon I was thinking too hard for my own good.

People could do that sometimes: say too little even when they knew it let others down. I wondered why both Grandma and Sa-wol couldn't tell me *more* instead. I didn't just want to know the *what*. I wanted to know the *why*. And if they couldn't tell me, I wished they could have told me the reason they wouldn't tell me.

By the time the taxi was in front of us, I was feeling prickly. I grabbed Sa-wol's arm and insisted, 'Let's go together.'

'I said I'd rather not –'

'If you can't be bothered to explain *why*, I'm not going to bother being considerate. I've had enough of guessing games.'

I hauled open the door of the taxi and shoved Sa-wol inside before he could protest. Then I climbed in after him and shut the door. It all happened in an instant, and before we knew it, the taxi was making its way to the temple.

It was only a five-minute drive, but Sa-wol pointedly stared out the other window. But what did I care? Now I had a comfortable ride and the cool, blessed air from the AC. Sa-wol was secretly enjoying it, too, I told myself –

'Sa-wol?'

There was something off about his breathing. His shoulders heaved, and I could hear him gasp as he drew his arm across his forehead. Cold sweat ran down his face.

'Are you all right?'

Sa-wol didn't say a thing. Soon he was gazing into the distance, and he hung his head until it was between his knees. He looked even worse than I had before I got into the taxi.

When he grasped at his chest and pounded desperately like a dying man, I finally screamed, 'Mr Driver! Please let us out here!'

The second the taxi came to a stop, Sa-wol collapsed onto the pavement. He was hyperventilating. 'What's going on? Are you all right?' I asked. 'Hold on, I'll call an ambulance –'

'Wait.'

Even as he struggled for breath, Sa-wol was perfectly calm. As if it had happened before. He reached for the yanggaeng I'd made him and took a bite. Clearly he wasn't hungry – so why? All I could do was wipe the sweat from his brow and apologize.

'I'm so sorry, Sa-wol. I shouldn't have done that,' I said, feeling guilty.

He looked up stiffly, like he was holding back his rage.

When he'd finished eating the yanggaeng, Sa-wol breathed a sigh of relief. His forehead was dry again, and when he pushed his hair out of his face, he looked like his usual self.

'Apology accepted,' he said. 'But no more taxis, all right?'

He was angry at me, I could tell. But he didn't take it out on me. Instead, he pushed ahead. I nodded firmly and held out my pinkie to promise I'd never force him into a taxi again.

'By the way,' I said, once the air had cleared, 'you devoured that yanggaeng earlier. What was that about?'

'You made it with the ingredients I delivered.'

'Yes, and?'

'I told you,' he said, 'my ingredients are special. I've filled them with spiritual powers – which means they can help me when my powers fail.'

'Your powers fail when you get into a taxi?'

Sa-wol looked up, pointing ahead with his jaw. 'We're here. Hongseoksa Temple.'

Once again, I noted, he'd ignored my question.

❀

We found the old monk in front of the Buddha in the main sanctuary. Again, he seemed to sense our presence on the serene temple grounds and turned in our direction.

I held out my shopping bag. 'Do you remember me, sir? Here, the yanggaeng is for you.'

The monk gave a smile as tranquil as the smiles of the statues that decorated Hongseoksa Temple.

Once he'd received the yellow cap, the monk held out an envelope of cash to compensate me for my work. He and Sa-wol didn't say a word to each other, only nodding quietly in recognition – not because they were on bad terms, but because they already knew each other so well.

Once I'd been paid, Sa-wol picked up a seat cushion and bowed before the statue of the Buddha. As I watched, the monk whispered into my ear, 'Today is his day of grace.'

'What does that mean?' I asked.

'Today, he commemorates the receiving of great grace from another. It is as important as a birthday to dear Sa-wol.'

The monk didn't give any details. What was the grace Sa-wol got, and why was it so important? Once again, I didn't think to ask the obvious questions. All I had were the blanks I hadn't filled.

There was something solemn about Sa-wol as he prostrated himself. 'Serious' wasn't a word I'd associate with him, but for the first time, I was reminded that he was a shaman by trade.

'Is this delivery all, then?' the monk asked, gently implying that I had a job to do.

'Oh! Actually, I had a question,' I said. 'Do you know about my grandmother's secret recipe for red chestnut yanggaeng?'

'Ah, so the cat has delivered the order.'

'Wait, how did you –'

The monk rummaged through a basket of knick-knacks as he replied, 'The secret is in the boulder on the hill behind the temple. You'll need some of its powder to bring out the colour in the jelly. But it's dangerous to go alone – you must take Sa-wol with you.'

'*Powdered stone?* But this is for eating!'

'Your grandmother should have left instructions for properly cleaning powdered stone in her recipe book,' the monk said, and pulled out a shovel.

We all love natural ingredients, but whoever heard of putting rock in yanggaeng? But I didn't think the monk was trying to prank me. I simply nodded and took the shovel. 'So where exactly is this boulder?'

The monk rose, his robes fluttering.

'W-wait! You didn't tell me where –'

The monk went on without looking back, without answering my question. He simply said:

'At times, the process of waiting is part of the answer itself.'

❀

As the sun set, Sa-wol guided me up the hill. He explained it was dangerous to go alone in the dark, and that he would stay with me until I safely came down the hill again.

'The monk told me today was a special day for you,' I said curiously. 'What happened, exactly?'

'That's none of your business,' he replied, his tone playful but evasive.

Sa-wol really was tough to get to know. It had been

weeks since we first met at the Hwawoldang, but I'd almost never seen anything behind the sly grin he always wore. I couldn't take much more of this. 'You only ever talk about the shop and Grandma,' I said. 'But you haven't told me anything about yourself, Mr Secrecy.'

Sa-wol only grinned.

I frowned. He didn't bother denying it! He didn't drop a single hint! Why wouldn't Sa-wol say *anything* at all?

The path up the hill was rugged and steep. There was no conversation after that, so I found my eyes drawn to the darkening skies between the foliage overhead. No one met us on the path, which made sense because our destination was a completely undeveloped cliffside.

'Beautiful, isn't it?' Sa-wol remarked.

Beyond the cliff, the fading twilight danced like the sea. Sa-wol stood proudly with his hands on his hips, explaining that he always paid this place a visit when he came to the temple.

I strained my eyes. I couldn't see the boulder anywhere.

'Take a closer look,' Sa-wol said, and I clambered around, examining the rocks under the trees. But all

I saw was grey and yellow. Sa-wol snickered at my desperation and pointed at the edge of the cliff.

I gave him a questioning look. 'Sa-wol, that's the cliffside.'

'Look closer.'

The flat plateau at the top of the cliff was covered in grass and wildflowers, with the crimson sunset painting the green grass a brilliant red. I looked down, and saw the dirt under my feet. I ran the toes of my shoe over the dirt.

It was below me.

'This whole cliff *is* the red boulder!' I exclaimed, clapping my hands. 'That's where the temple name comes from! Hongseoksa *means* "red stone temple"!'

Sa-wol gave me a thumbs-up. 'Once upon a time, this cliff caught fire,' he said. 'But the fire was extinguished by a virtuous blind man, and the boulder god granted the man and this cliff great spiritual influence. There's something special about the stone here, even now.'

He pointed at the shovel I'd brought.

'I'll be collecting the powdered stone.'

'What? No, but—'

'It's dangerous, Yeon-hwa,' he said. 'This *is* a cliffside, you know.'

'But I . . .'

Sa-wol didn't let me finish. He snatched my shovel, strode to the edge of the cliff, and scraped at the ground. Even half-cast in twilight, his face masked red on one side, he looked as calm as ever. For some reason, I didn't feel like thanking him. Sa-wol was always the one taking the lead, without explaining a thing.

'Let me do this,' I finally stated. 'I'm the one making the yanggaeng. This is part of my job.'

'It's dangerous, Yeon-hwa,' Sa-wol said again.

'I don't need your help with this.'

'Don't be stubborn.'

Sa-wol was doing me a *favour* by collecting the powdered stone. So why was I so angry? I snatched the shovel back from him. 'This is *my* job,' I repeated. 'I can do this.'

'There's no need to lose your temper, Yeon-hwa. I just want to help –'

'I don't believe you,' I retorted. 'There's some secret method to collecting the powder, isn't there? *Another* secret for you to keep from me?'

Sa-wol insisted, 'No, there's no secret here, Yeon-hwa. The cliffside gets windy, and –'

I'd had enough of his excuses. I was sick and tired

of speculating about everything he never bothered to explain. Pulling Sa-wol back, I marched up to the edge myself and squatted to scrape at the ground. I'd never been so stubborn before, but everything Sa-wol did and said today made me furious. I felt like a stranger to myself. Behind me, Sa-wol raised his voice, claiming he'd just wanted to help.

He was right. Why was I getting mad at him, when I should have been thanking him?

I didn't know why I said the next thing that came to mind:

'Sa-wol, can you *please* just let me do what I want?'

There was a gust of wind.

I smelled something familiar, something that reminded me of the Hwawoldang. The smell filled my nose and my eyes, and in that instant, I lost my balance. My feet stumbled, and my body arched forward and back. The distant ground whipped into view. And when my mind sensed the sheer distance of the drop, my heart pounded madly.

Then Sa-wol's hand was wrapped around my arm, and he was hauling me back. 'I *told* you it was dangerous!' he snapped.

My heart was still racing as he scolded me. And nothing would slow it down.

'Now stand back and let *me* get the powdered stone,' Sa-wol said angrily.

I couldn't take that lying down. 'You know what, Sa-wol? You're right. But that doesn't mean you can order me around like that. I told you! I never *asked* for your help.'

'You almost *fell*.'

'Who cares?'

'What is going on with you today?' Sa-wol asked in disbelief. 'Why do you have to argue with everything I do?'

'*Argue?*' I repeated, my pulse racing again, and not because of the brush with death. Dusk rested fully on Sa-wol, setting him afire. I stood across from him, dark in the shadows of the trees. 'If I was arguing, it's only because *you* wouldn't listen to a thing I said.'

'How is it not obvious that doing *anything* at the edge of a *cliff* is dangerous work?'

'It's not just about the cliff!' I retorted.

I didn't have Sa-wol's fire. I didn't have his mysterious ability to draw people's attention and curiosity, to make people wonder intently about me. That was why he never tried to get close to me the way I tried to get close to him. That was all I was to him: someone he needed to give instructions to.

All this time, I'd had nothing but questions and theories. I was kept in the dark about so many things in my life. I was left to rely completely on others, like Grandma and Sa-wol, with no explanation about the things that affected me.

It felt humiliating.

I'd hated it for a very long time.

'I don't like the fact that you know so much more than me,' I said.

'But that's only natural, Yeon-hwa. I've known about the Hwawoldang far longer than you, since I was young—'

'Look, don't treat me like Grandma did, okay?'

I was sick of myself. All these years, I'd done nothing but listen and do what I was told. I'd never done or learned anything about myself. All the frustrations I'd built up over time finally blew up when Sa-wol, just like Grandma, brushed off my questions.

'I want to *know* why you hate taking the taxi,' I said. 'I want to know how you know my grandma, and what exactly you did for her. I want to know how you're connected to this temple. I'm tired of being kept in the dark. I want *answers*, Sa-wol. I want to know the truth!'

For a time, Sa-wol stood in stunned silence. The

sun dipped further and further into the horizon until it was a sliver in the distance, but the longest silence of our lives went on.

Then the wind stopped.

'I want you to promise me,' Sa-wol finally said, 'that when you learn the truth . . . you won't resent me.'

He pulled out the little bell he carried around. The evening light shone mystically on its surface, and I knew I was being handed a memento of the dead. But I didn't hesitate. I put my hand on the bell.

❀

My second name was Sa-wol.

Hongseoksa Temple had few visitors. No one wandered in by accident. Only two sorts of people ever came through the gates: people who knew what they wanted – fame, fortune, health or happiness – and a few people who knew what they wanted to be rid of. This second group of people came to the temple to drop off the things that made them unhappy.

I was dropped off at the entrance on one sunny day in April.

I must have had another name before, but because

no one had any way of knowing what, I was taken in by the temple and given a second name: Sa-wol, for the month they found me in.

'Say, O-wol, d'you think Granny is coming again today?'

'Uh-huh. Remember she promised to bring us yanggaeng again?'

'I can't wait!'

'Me too!'

O-wol was dropped off the year before me. We grew up like brothers and were raised as child monks by the temple, to be cared for until we came of age. It was only later that I realized the temple's charity was the reason irresponsible visitors came to treat it as a dumping ground.

The temple didn't have much in the way of toys, but we always had something – someone – to look forward to. 'Granny' was the owner of a traditional sweetshop, and when she came to the temple to be paid for her work, she made sure to bring treats for us children. She brought a different treat each time, and soon she was our own Santa Claus.

When she came to the temple, she called loudly, 'Sa-wol! O-wol!' and we would scamper over like a pair of puppies. Granny would pull us into a warm hug with shopping bags still in hand.

We sat together at the deserted gate one day, chomping on the chestnut yanggaeng she'd brought. 'Don't tell the monks I brought you these,' Granny warned with a smile, and O-wol – who was always the more outgoing one – replied playfully, 'Only if you give us one more!'

Granny grinned and pulled out another stick of yanggaeng. O-wol cheered and bit down on the yanggaeng, replying with a full mouth, 'These are so red, and they taste even better than the normal ones!'

'It's because they're packed with spiritual energies from the red boulder,' Granny said. 'The powdered stone from the cliff is the secret ingredient,' she whispered.

Granny once told us that she had a granddaughter just about our age. I never saw her, but I could picture how Granny's face must look when she was with the girl: the same loving smile she had when she watched us eat her treats. Part of me wished I could live that girl's life, getting to see that smile every single day.

'How are you liking your yanggaeng?'

'It's so good!'

'I don't know. Wouldn't you prefer something like cake, or cream-filled buns?'

'Well, we've never tried those.'

I wondered, though, if the girl knew that look of sympathy we sometimes saw on Granny's face.

Granny ruffled our hair and ran her hands gently on our backs as we enjoyed our treats, but she couldn't hide the sadness in her eyes. She told us about a friend she'd grown up with, back in the countryside. Her friend had loved sweets, just like us, and had always wanted to try one of those 'chocolate cakes' they sold in the cities. She'd cut out pictures of cakes from the magazines and paste them into her diary with big dreams for her future. But the friend, Granny said, died of an illness before she was twenty.

We reminded her of that girl, Granny would say, and used the word 'wistfulness' when she tried to explain.

I was too young to understand what the word really meant.

'Well, if you like the yanggaeng so much,' Granny said, 'why don't you come down to the shop once in a while?'

With that, Granny took our hands and went to

the monks, asking for permission to take us to her shop. The monks first apologized – because it could not be easy to babysit two unruly children at once – but thanked her for her kindness. We left the temple for the first time in ages.

As we went down the street, Granny asked O-wol, 'What would you like to eat the most, O-wol dear?'

'Um, can you make us one of those "cakes" you told us about?'

'Of course, sweetheart. I'll make as much as you can eat.'

'Hooray!'

I held her right hand, and O-wol held her left. We didn't see Granny often, and we hadn't spoken to her that much, but she was one of the few people who wanted to show us the outside world. We loved her for it.

'And what about you, Sa-wol dear?'

'Um . . .'

I thought about all the western desserts I'd never had the chance to try. Whipped cream was supposed to be white and soft, and it was supposed to melt so quickly in your mouth that you couldn't chew it. And marshmallows, those were supposed to be squishy like well-dried blankets. And chocolates, and vanilla, and tiramisu . . . there was so much I wanted to try. I wanted to ask for everything.

But I'd grown up faster than other kids my age, and I knew I couldn't pay for dessert. From the moment I learned that my parents had abandoned me at the temple to be raised by the monks, I'd always felt ashamed in front of other people. I wasn't quite old enough to define the sense of 'indebtedness', so I never said a word about this mysterious feeling.

I didn't manage to give Granny an answer before we arrived at her shop.

Granny went to the fridge and brought out ready-made cake. She thawed it, warmed it up, and soon our mouths were covered in whipped cream. I couldn't believe it. The cake looked like bread, but it was so soft, and when I stuck a fork into a big chunk and took a bite out of my piece, it seemed to shrink in my mouth instantly.

'How do you boys like it?'
'It's so good, Granny!'
'Then let's try these, too,' Granny offered, taking out shop-bought marshmallows and tiramisu – treats I'd never mentioned out loud but had always wondered about.

'I have spiritual powers, you know,' Granny explained. 'They let me see into your hearts.'

'Wow! Are you a ghost, Granny?'

Granny laughed out loud when we said that. She was no ghost, but with her special powers, she opened our eyes to a whole new world. O-wol and I couldn't get enough of these shocking new sweets. The flavours and textures were seared into our memories forever. Sometimes, we broke into ridiculous dances and cheers, and Granny burst into laughter again when she saw O-wol jump in his seat with every spoonful of tiramisu.

'There are so many sweets and exciting things out there,' Granny said to us. 'So enjoy the world to its fullest. Don't you ever live like you're prisoners.'

'Are we prisoners now?'

'No, not at all! Right now, you're still growing up at the temple so that you can be free someday.'

'FREEDOM!'

After feasting on desserts and Granny's advice, we slapped our full bellies and got ready to go back to the temple. Granny even packed up some cookies for the monks who raised us, specially made for them without any animal products.

'I can't wait to try these!' O-wol cried, darting out of the shop. We were both children, and we never got tired. O-wol remembered the monks, too, promising to save them some, and challenged me to a race. We sprinted up the mountain to the temple, ignoring Granny calling to us to wait for her.

It was evening, but the sun hadn't quite set. The world glowed red like it was covered in crimson silk, exactly the hue of the red cliff behind the temple building. The hue was so beautiful that it distracted a taxi driver, whose eyes were pulled into his rear-view mirror.

'Boys, wait!'

Then I felt a dense, metallic impact. O-wol and I rose horribly together into the air.

'Sa-wol! O-wol!'

There was a loud thud, and I felt something run down my head. Cookies were strewn all around us, broken to bits. All I could think was how sad the monks would be to miss out on them.

Then we were falling, O-wol and me, and the last thing I saw was my brother's face, his eyes wide open as he landed on the pavement.

I pulled away quickly from Sa-wol's bell. He explained what had happened next.

By the time Grandma had reached them, the boys were barely clinging to life. Grandma saved them by channelling her powers into them, preventing their souls from leaving their bodies. Sa-wol and O-wol were saved by a miracle, and although they struggled for a time with the after-effects, they eventually regained their health. Grandma's powers lingered with the boys, though, and Sa-wol became a shaman, while O-wol, who didn't want to follow that path, moved overseas as soon as he was old enough.

'But there was a problem,' Sa-wol explained. 'There's a sort of law concerning life and death. If one death is prevented, another must take its place. Because your grandmother intervened in our fates, she was punished: with a car accident, at that.'

'. . . No . . .'

Sa-wol pulled out his wallet, and showed me the picture he kept inside.

A picture of a younger me, which Grandma had taken.

'I always felt indebted to you because of that. So when your grandmother entrusted you to me, I felt free for the first time in my life. I'd been waiting so long for this chance . . . this chance to pay back what I owed.'

When he realized that my parents had ultimately died in place of himself and O-wol, Sa-wol was wracked with guilt. Grandma, too, agonized for the rest of her years about causing the deaths of her daughter and son-in-law with her impulsive choice.

Was that the reason, then? Did she feel so guilty for my parents' deaths that she never really explained what had happened? Even as she lay dying?

I didn't know what to think. Sa-wol . . . caused my parents' deaths? I thought of the price that had been paid. In that instant, I loathed him.

'I'm sorry it took so long to tell you.'

'But how . . .'

Sa-wol had only been helping me as a way to pay me back for my parents' lives. It was infuriating. Awful. But I couldn't blame him for it. Not completely. Sa-wol hadn't asked anyone to save him. No one was guilty here. But then how was anyone supposed to take responsibility? I'd lost my *parents* at a young age. Lost the years I should have had with them.

'. . . I'm going on ahead,' I said, turning quickly aside, even as Sa-wol tried to grab my arm. I didn't want to speak to him anymore.

'Please, Yeon-hwa. Don't blame your grandmother.'

I didn't want to hear him, either. I gathered up the powdered stone and the shovel, and rushed back down the slopes.

❦

Back at the Hwawoldang, all I could do was stare blankly as I fiddled with the red bean paste.

In the booklet, I'd found the instructions for washing the powdered stone, just like the monk had explained. Although I took in the instructions and my hands followed them, my mind was elsewhere. I mechanically stirred together the purified powder with the bean paste.

When the completed yanggaeng jelly took on a bright red hue, I knew I'd succeeded in making the Hwawoldang's specialty recipe. But for some reason, I wasn't happy. I was overwhelmed by so many emotions that I felt numb. All I could do was wrap up the yanggaeng and wait for the customer to come pick up their order.

'Meow.'

The black cat arrived just before midnight. I knelt in front of her and held out the packaged red chestnut yanggaeng, but she sat there, staring up into my face.

'You know, Kitty? I found out something awful while I was preparing this recipe.'

I wished I'd never asked. Ignorance really was bliss. All I had now was a terrible truth, the knowledge of a past I could never change. I wondered if things would have been better if Grandma had told me when I was young – if I'd had time to work through it all and move on. Maybe if she had, I would have been over it by now.

At the moment, though? All my emotions swirled together, and the only thing I could make out was resentment. Was Grandma the reason I'd lost so much?

'Meeeeow.'

The cat head-butted the top of my foot, as if trying to comfort me.

'I don't understand.'

I'd feel more alive if I were buried in concrete, I thought. I breathed in, but I felt choked. With a sigh, I hung my head – and saw a bright light.

The cat seemed to be glowing. And it changed shape, getting larger and larger, until it was the shape of a person dressed in a white hanbok, squatting just like me . . .

'How are you, Yeon-hwa?'

Grandma.

'Now you know the truth, dear.'

First came shock. But the resentment wasn't far behind.

'Grandma, how could you?'

'I'm sorry, dear,' Grandma replied. 'At the time, all I knew was that I wanted to save those boys. I never realized what a terrible price I would have to pay. I wanted to take responsibility, to at least make sure you had everything you needed, but I just couldn't bring myself to tell you the truth. I am so, so sorry, Yeon-hwa.'

I was indignant. 'I don't *want* an explanation! What about my *parents*? What about *me*? You couldn't have told me any of this sooner? Why make me wait all these years?'

'Yeon-hwa. I was afraid.'

Grandma's dark eyes brimmed with tears. I'd never seen them that way. I knew that she was not making excuses for her actions.

Afraid. It was such a simple word, but so heavy, and so powerful that it kicked up a typhoon in my heart. The Grandma I remembered was never afraid – *I* was the scared one, always terrified that Grandma would abandon me if I asked too many questions. Grandma had always been so difficult, had never been open, and had been an eternal secret-keeper.

But now for the first time she was just another person. Just as afraid as me.

'I kept running away, Yeon-hwa, because I was afraid and selfish. I could never blame you for resenting me, dear. How could you not, when I waited until after I'd *died* to tell you the truth, and through someone else?'

'And *that's* why you never tried to get close to me?'

'I was terrified that my own granddaughter might hate me.'

What the heck. We were two peas in a pod. The ghost in front of me was never as strong as she'd looked, and now I couldn't bear to stab her with my resentment. How could I, when we were so alike?

But I still had something to say:

'Things could have been different if you'd told me sooner.'

'I know,' Grandma replied. 'But some people are just born that way. They can't bring themselves to be honest. I spent all these years hoping for a change, and look at me now. I *have* been changed, but only after death. All I can say, Yeon-hwa, is that I hope you live differently.'

Then, after a moment's hesitation, Grandma wrapped her arms around me. She was still so warm.

'Yeon-hwa, I want you to be the person I never was. Listen to the people who can't speak for themselves, hear their voices, and stand up for them. I know you can do it.'

When she pulled away, I saw my own face in hers. I recognized the regrets, too, so much like mine. Grandma reached into her sleeve and pulled out a mirror. Inside, I saw Mum and Dad, both smiling. They looked just as young as I remembered them, but for some reason, the picture didn't seem to be from the past.

'We're all together in the world beyond,' Grandma explained. 'We work together to welcome the dead. And your parents, you know, want you to be happy.'

'What about you, Grandma? Do . . . do you want me to be happy?'

'Of *course* I do.'

Was it all leading up to this final confession? Was this why Grandma had made even her own death part of her waiting? I'd spent my life resenting the secrets people kept from me, but I realized that there was a reason for every secret. I thought of my own actions. I remembered how I'd failed to care for others, and thought back to Grandma's words.

Then it was midnight, the time when the dead prepared to leave the shop. The moon hung pale and clear in the sky, pressing for the mercy of the living.

I knew that there was nothing else I could do. Grandma asking for my forgiveness, me forgiving her, and the whole process of overcoming my hatred and loathing – it had all happened like it was destiny. I realized that I didn't need to always understand *everything* to send someone off with a smile. All it really took was a bit of courage. The courage to accept a person, fears and all.

I took Grandma's hand.

'. . . Thank you, Yeon-hwa.'

Finally, with my forgiveness and blessings, Grandma gave me a nod of happiness. This would be our final farewell.

May your steps be free of grief as you pass.

May the wistful memories you leave be filled with all the warmth we never shared in life.

'Goodbye, Grandma.'

'Be well, and enjoy the rest of your life, Yeon-hwa.

The dead who remember you still pray for your happiness.'

Even as she faded into a cloud of smoke, scattering in the breeze, Grandma didn't lose her form. She went on, step by step, still herself. All my questions and waiting had led me here. We wished each other well. Only after she had passed did Grandma become the guidepost of my life as she sparkled among the stars.

❀

After that unexpected goodbye, I started closing up shop. I felt a bit better, and thought some yanggaeng might do me good, too. The leftovers tasted sweet – but not too sweet – with a nutty flavour and the scent of forests from the powdered stone. It was perfectly unique. The powers imbued in the ingredients seemed to make even the texture soft and welcoming.

It was too bad I'd only brought enough powder for that one batch. I couldn't go back to Hongseoksa Temple now, not after the way I stormed off –

'Haven't closed up yet, I see.'

Speak of the devil. Sa-wol had opened the door so timidly he didn't seem himself. He looked like he wanted to continue the conversation from before.

Not me, though. Getting closure with Grandma didn't mean Sa-wol was automatically off the hook.

'Well, it's closed now,' I said firmly, intentionally avoiding his gaze as I went through the motions of cleaning.

Sa-wol, though? He looked embarrassed, but he wouldn't leave.

'I wanted to apologize to you,' he told me.

I didn't answer. He was only here to make excuses for himself, I was sure of it.

'I'm sorry I wasn't honest with you from the start,' said Sa-wol. 'I know that nothing I say is going to make you feel better, but I wanted to apologize anyway.'

It was so weird, seeing him without his usual swagger, running his hands down his face like he was anxious for once.

I wasn't heartless enough to snap at someone in the middle of a heartfelt apology.

There was a cool gust of wind, and the fury that had followed me all the way down the mountain began to dissipate.

How strange. When he told me the truth, I'd hated him. Resented him. My parents were dead, and now my grandmother was gone, leaving behind me, Sa-wol and his brother. Who was I supposed to blame? I forgave Grandma, so should I take out the rest of my emotions – my resentment – on Sa-wol?

And then what? What would happen after that?

'All this time,' Sa-wol said as I stood silent, 'I'd lived my life like an apology. I wanted to say sorry for what I'd taken away by continuing to live, Yeon-hwa. And I know I could never pay you back for what you lost. No one could. But please, let me do *something*.'

'That's very selfish of you,' I said.

'I suppose it is,' he replied.

'You're only apologizing to make yourself feel better.'

'I only want to help preserve the Hwawoldang, and your grandmother's work –'

I couldn't take it anymore. I exploded. 'I'm *not* my grandmother!' I cried with fists clenched, the words pouring out like air from a burst balloon. 'I'm *me*! Not "granddaughter of Lim Yun-ok", not the "heir to the Hwawoldang", just *me*! Hong Yeon-hwa!'

Then I realized: I wasn't talking to Sa-wol. Or to Grandma or my parents.

This was all stuff I'd needed to say to *myself*.

I'd always wanted to be *me*. I didn't want to

dedicate my life to carrying on someone's legacy, or to helping other people for their sake. I'm sure those things would be meaningful and fulfilling in their own way. But not until I'd found my true self. Grandma's silence hadn't just hidden the truth about my parents. I'd never had the chance to find myself because the person who was supposed to be closest to me rarely spoke to me.

I would spend my adult life trying to make up for that lost chance. It all felt so daunting. Too much work for me to even consider carrying on someone else's work.

'It's getting late,' I said, pushing Sa-wol out the door. Would sending him away make me feel better? 'You should go home.'

But Sa-wol never once looked away. '*I understand*, Yeon-hwa.'

'What do you mean?'

'I've never seen you as someone else's legacy.'

I couldn't believe my ears. 'But you just said you wanted to preserve the shop, and Grandma's work,' I said, glaring. Why did he have to be so dense? Why couldn't he understand that I *hadn't* agreed to this conversation in the dead of night just to hear his platitudes?

'And that's also true. I know that *you're* the one keeping the Hwawoldang now.'

'Yes, I've heard all this already.'

'Then how many times do I have to repeat myself?' Sa-wol shot back.

He held out a plastic bag. It was filled with powdered stone from the mountain.

Did . . . did he stay behind to collect more? For me?

'I want to stay and support *you*, Yeon-hwa. I know this sounds selfish, but that's the whole reason I offered to help keep the shop running and to carry on your grandmother's legacy. Helping you was always my first priority. This is how I want to use the life I was granted.'

Moonlight shone in Sa-wol's eyes, filled with a vivid gleam. A gleam I'd never seen in the eyes of the dead.

'I want you to give me a chance,' Sa-wol pleaded. 'A chance to answer any and all questions you might have. Please, Yeon-hwa.'

All this time, I'd thought I'd lived only for others, never getting answers from anyone. But here was Sa-wol, trying so hard to be the exception. The moment he called my name, offering to spend his life giving me *answers*, the world seemed to come into bloom.

It was a promise that I would never spend my days drifting alone again. I could spread my wings and fly out into the world.

Sa-wol came back into the Hwawoldang, went to the counter, and bent down over the floor. And in the blink of an eye, he'd dislodged a squeaky tile to reveal a hidden compartment.

Inside was a small, locked chest. He nodded.

'It's time,' said Sa-wol. 'You're the true master of the Hwawoldang now.'

I placed my brand-new world atop his outstretched hand.

We were finally, truly, working together.

7

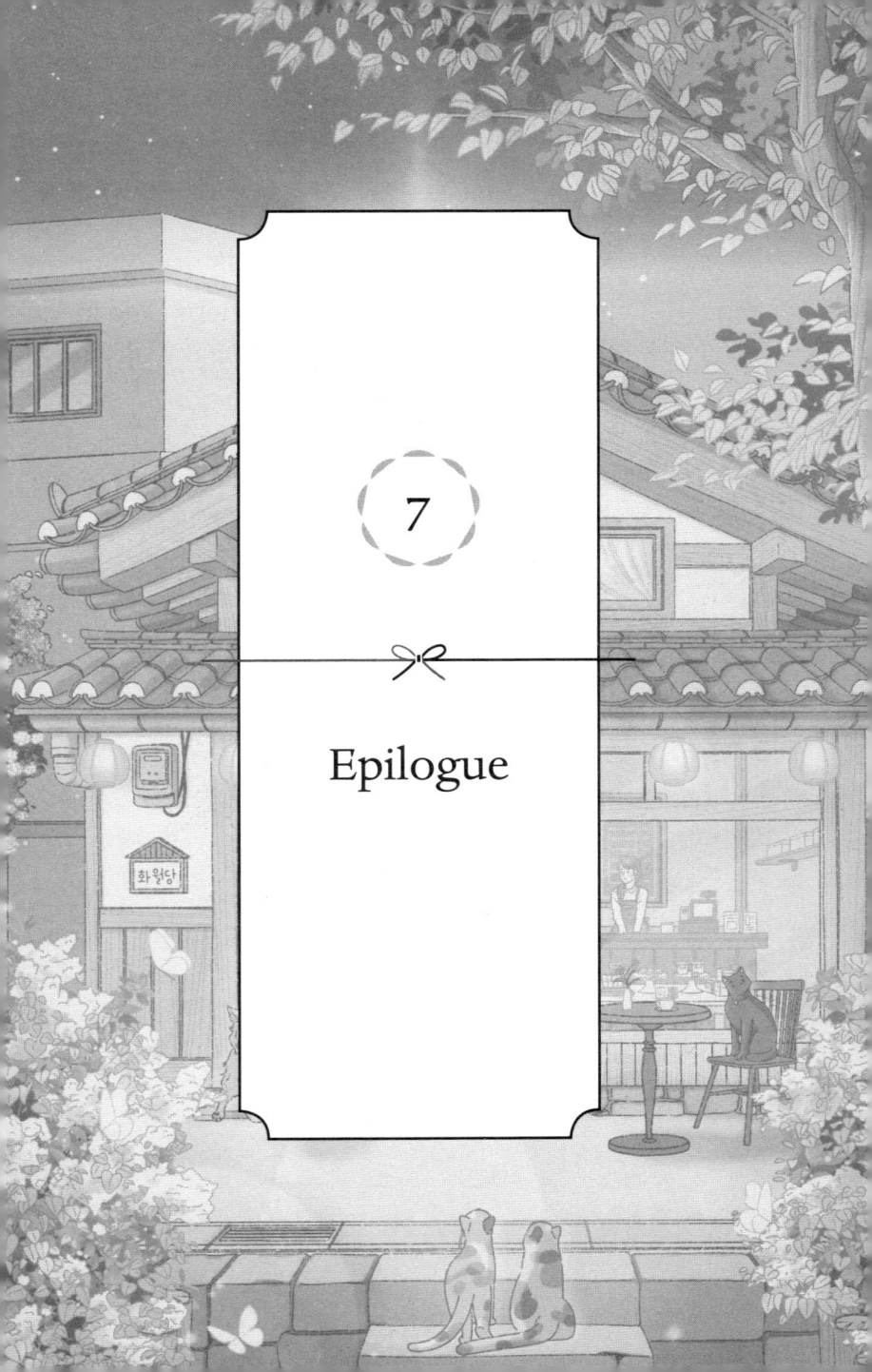

Epilogue

After Grandma left with her yanggaeng, the dead stopped coming as much as before. Sa-wol guessed it was because the shop's powers waned when Grandma passed on. Other shops would keep on catering to the dead, he said, and as long as they went on doing business, the spirits of the departed would be taken good care of.

But there was a problem: if we lost our dead customers – and the objects they left behind for trading in to the temple – I had almost no income. The Hwawoldang was in *deep* trouble. Since there was no way I'd sell off the shop now, I had to get to work fast.

I threw myself into the world of small business ownership.

I opened up the shop in the morning now

and started marketing in earnest. Thankfully, customers – live ones – came in droves.

'Excuse me, do you have any more of the five-piece red yanggaeng sets?'

'I'm sorry, we sold out in the afternoon.'

'Oh, shucks. This is my third time here, and you always sell out so quick.'

'Then would you like to make a reservation? The yanggaeng are ready for pick-up at eleven in the morning.'

The Hwawoldang's signature red chestnut yanggaeng was a huge hit on Instagram. Customers in their twenties and thirties packed the shop every day, and although it took some getting used to, I couldn't complain. It was nice to see the shop so full of life. I knew Grandma would be happy, if she could see this.

'Sa-wol, I need a hundred more grams of the powdered stone by tomorrow.'

'*Again?* Tell me to carry the whole mountain here, why don't you?'

'Is that any way to talk to your employer?'

'I take it back,' Sa-wol said melodramatically. 'If I'd known you'd pay peanuts for my help, I would never have made that heartfelt plea. Have you considered giving me a raise, Yeon-hwa? I'd love to get a pair of those neckband headphones everyone's raving about.'

'Not with that debt still hanging over our heads,' I said with a playful sigh, foisting an armful of wrapping papers for him to make gift boxes with.

Grandma's secret? It turned out to be a deed kept in that secret box beneath the floor tiles. Apparently Hongseoksa Temple had given her part of the temple's lands – the red cliff, specifically – in place of a cash payment once. The lawyer congratulated me, because it was going to come in handy paying down the debt.

Unfortunately, we discovered that the whole area was recently designated a protected greenbelt. There was no selling that parcel of land, at least not anytime soon. So I was still a hundred million won in debt, and that gave me all the motivation in the world to make the Hwawoldang the biggest name in traditional sweets.

But the funny thing? I wasn't upset. I was improving my skills by leaps and bounds each day. Sa-wol's special ingredients even gave our customers great luck – according to the social media posts, anyway – which meant I was placing 'SOLD OUT' signs on the shelves almost as soon as they were stocked. I went home exhausted every day, but it felt good to know that I was a proper, working adult who could pull her own weight. Two times my weight, since I was paying Sa-wol, too.

'Yes, could I reserve one box of the red yang-gaeng, then?' asked the customer. 'I can't be here tomorrow, so I'll leave my husband's name, if that's all right. And one more thing . . .' The woman trailed off, knitting her brow. She gestured wildly, drawing circles in the air with her finger. 'What was it again? It was brown, and salty . . .'

'Soy sauce dango, you mean?' I asked.

'No, no. Oh, it's on the tip of my tongue . . . you know, the flat, crispy treats . . . I used to eat them up when I was little . . .'

Yi-ryeong burst into the shop, interrupting the woman's train of thought. 'What the heck, Yeon-hwa?' she complained with a pout. 'Today's my day off, you can't make me run errands for you!' But she held up a shopping bag anyway. Inside was something I'd been meaning to bring to the Hwawoldang for a while.

The customer went back to thinking, and I grinned playfully at Yi-ryeong. 'Sorry. I just keep forgetting to bring it with me.'

I took the shopping bag and pulled out its contents – a flower-print dress. The payment from the first customer, which the monk had declined. It was supposed to still have a role to play. I'd thought it would be a nice piece of memorabilia to hang on the wall while I waited for that fateful moment. I held up the dress against all manner of surfaces, trying to see what worked best –

'I've got it!' the customer exclaimed. 'It was *jeonbyeong crackers*! . . . Hm?'

I held my breath. That moment came sooner than I'd thought.

The customer came up to me, her eyes wide. 'Excuse me, but can I see that dress?'

I held it up for her, and as the customer's eyes took in the bright yellow hydrangeas blooming across the fabric, shock and grief rose to her face. Sa-wol seemed to realize what was happening, and quietly clasped his hands in prayer behind her. Serenity blanketed the once-busy Hwawoldang.

'. . . How . . . how did this end up here . . . ?' the customer breathed in awe.

'It's yours, if you'd like,' I said, remembering Grandma's words.

Life was a fleeting moment, but our bonds would

last forever. We were meant to say goodbye with a smile. The magical connections that tied us together might also pull us apart, but that wasn't the end. The Hwawoldang was the crossroads between the living and the dead. With a sense of gratitude for all the new bonds I'd formed at Grandma's shop, I took the customer's hands warmly in mine.

'She wants you to be happy,' I said. 'Always.'